CW01509749

The C

The Coca Man

P. Dersen

The Pentland Press Limited
Edinburgh • Cambridge • Durham • USA

First published in 1997 by
The Pentland Press Ltd.
1 Hutton Close
South Church
Bishop Auckland
Durham

British Library Cataloguing in Publication Data.
A Catalogue record for this book is available
from the British Library.

ISBN 1 85821 468 8

Typeset by CBS, Felixstowe, Suffolk
Printed and bound by Antony Rowe Ltd., Chippenham

I wish to dedicate this novel to the officers of Customs and Excise, who despite the constraints of Government deregulation, operate fearlessly in the fight to contain the criminal actions of drug smugglers and their hirelings. It is surely time they were given the extra manpower and equipment required to eliminate those Merchants of misery, allowing our youth to develop in such a way that drug addiction becomes a rarity and no longer a rave.

ACKNOWLEDGEMENT

I would like to express my thanks and appreciation to the Herbert family for the work they undertook in the printing of the manuscript prior to publication.

THE COCA MAN

CHARACTERS

Mr Wil Ling
Mr Sorenson, Author
Ignatius Lucius Chancitt
El Chanceet
Editor
Hector Macdonald, Lawyer
Rogerson
Pierre le Blanc
Neal Munro
Neal Munro Jnr.
Niki
Collette
Tom Smart
Dowager Duchess Marie Louise
Nicholas Quarefellow, Lawyer
Jehu Cristo
Big Mac
Pepe

CHAPTER 1

Should my body be found dead, under circumstances which indicate foul play, I have ensured that the Forensic Department and the Coroner concerned will be able to identify me. To expedite identification I have had tattooed on the inner aspect of my right thigh, close to the most vulnerable part known to man, a work of art signifying that when alive I was known as Wil Ling. You may think it strange I should take such precautions, but with a name like Wil Ling you can well understand that people became confused when I introduced myself; many thought I was agreeing to some odious task that no other person would volunteer to perform.

I had seriously considered at one time having my first name changed to Unwil, but as it sounded rather Gaelic and I am fair skinned, I decided against it. I don't think it made much difference. I have managed to court trouble on numerous occasions and have survived by learning to merge unseen into the background, unannounced and discreetly quiet. However, I must admit that when I was young with no father to guide me, I believed the word Conservative had something to do with protecting rain forests, but later I discovered it referred to the protection of a way of life. It envisaged middle and upper class people, who, ordained to govern, taught us to 'conserve' our position in life.

For the benefit of all it was important that the working class should strive to conserve their skills and ability to work hard, and that those who governed us should spare no effort in conserving the wealth of our nation. After leaving school it did not take long to make me realise that the Conservatives had conveniently forgotten to mention that 'our nation' meant 'our class'. What a confidence trick to foist on a working class lad with the unfortunate name of Wil Ling!

Having an acute sense of humour, I quickly learned how to survive; without kicking my fellow workers in the teeth. I know now that I have been fortunate, never having felt the urge to join the 'rat race' for wealth and power. Health was my first consideration; to me this meant movement, embodying as it does a clear mind in a healthy body. It would appear that most of us seek happiness, and as it has been suggested that happiness is in essence a state of mind, then it surely follows that the pursuance of health is paramount.

There can be little doubt that my life has been one of movement. Starting my life as an apprentice engineer, I ultimately qualified as a journeyman. The term is appropriate, for I soon discovered that I had to journey from place to place if I wished to be paid wages in any way commensurate with my skills. At the time the Scottish fitter and turner, like the Scottish soldier, gave the best performance at rock bottom prices. Believing in the dignity of man and a 'fair wage' packet, it seemed only natural that I should find myself functioning as a Shop Steward's Convener. It was not long before I was again journeying. Only this time as I approached a 'likely' place of employment, a 'wee black ball' had rolled forward, completely blocking my entrance.

Since then I have done many things, ending up latterly in the newspaper industry. For five years I operated as foreign correspondent for the *Daily Truth* and covered events in the U.S.A. and South America. It was an assignment in Colombia that put me at hazard – they called it the 'Cocaine Scandal' at the time.

I had been rather caustic in dispatches concerning the nefarious and underhand activities of United States agents in Central and South America, but despite this I had made friends with American correspondents, even secret agents, who, having to face the sharp end of misdirected policy, were often inclined to agree with me and gave succour when required. On one occasion I was rescued from the clutches of a cocaine gang; it was the opportune intervention of American secret agents armed with machine guns that saved me. Although mindful of the service they rendered, my thoughts are still with the old man who had been instructed to guard me. The gang boss had made it clear that 'el Gringo' would surely die if he did not make available information regarding the whereabouts and plans of American agents in the area.

The conditions of imprisonment were almost intolerable. An old dark skinned ugly Colombian peasant fed me scraps surreptitiously. I would most certainly have died had he not felt pity for my unhappy and desperate plight. Beauty is indeed in the eye of the beholder and the old man, almost cadaverous in appearance, was to me a symbol of salvation. I was guarded night and day by the old man and a younger man of the gang. For most of the time they sat facing me, their rifles held lightly across their thighs. The old man, evidently in charge, issued instructions from time to time, leaving us together. Although an old man, he had never travelled far from his mountain homeland. The coca shrub had played a dominant part in his life, but his main interest was in knowing what life was like in the world beyond the Colombian mountains. There was a mutual exchange of information between us, he learning something of the world beyond his forest home, and I being made privy to his background as a Colombian peasant.

His early childhood had been spent as a help on the farm, tending the goats and running errands for his mother, a poor farm servant. He had never seen his father, but his mother had often referred to him despairingly as a 'gringo' who had mysteriously disappeared when the State Police had raided nearby farms and cocaine distilleries in the forest. They were to have been married by the Catholic priest in the area; unfortunately the police had arrived before the ceremony and his father had either disappeared or been abducted by the local cocaine clan. Whatever the truth of the matter, his mother had told him that his father was an American 'gringo' called Chanceet.

Although an American, he had claimed he was the son of an 'Inglese', a member of a noble family who had probably been glad to be rid of him. I wondered was this man 'Chanceet' really a 'remittance man' sent to America by an old English family, whose escutcheon had been severely dented. It was a conversation I was unable to develop, for the American agents had intervened, probably saving me from extinction.

It was not long after this that Head Office summoned me back to London. Many changes had taken place. The paper I represented, the *Daily Truth,* had now been renamed the *Morning Sun.* The British people had allowed themselves to be saddled with a government pledged to a policy of de-regulation, which to the poorest section of the community meant instant de-humanisation. The editor explained to me that we were into what was already being called the 'greedy eighties'. Many of our readers had been bitten by the greed bug, and feeling uncomfortable with the 'truth', were now deserting the cause and the paper. Although the paper's policy would remain the same, presentation would be different and changing the label would avert extinction. His theory was that as the 'free for all' developed and unemployment rose dramatically, there would be an increasing demand for information and redress.

A time would come when even those in the 'higher' echelons would be tossed off the 'gravy train' and join forces with the have-nots and the unemployed in ridding society of a government devoid of humanity and social policy, a government only interested in its own survival and having as its attitude 'the devil take the hindmost'. 'You see,' he said, 'scandals sell newspapers and you, my boy, have proved you now have the prowess of a top investigative journalist.' As I smiled at his blandishment he was quick to remind me that what I was being offered was, in a way, just as dangerous as ferreting out cocaine smugglers in South America. My salary as such would remain the same, but the bonuses relative to the scandals I unearthed would more than pay for my style of life, provided, of course, that I lived long enough to enjoy them.

Within a few days I knew my editor had not exaggerated. Greed was certainly running in top gear, with one of the most inept governments of the century fuelling the process. We had more 'self made' millionaires and more criminals, many of them a combination of both. Unemployment, poverty and deprivation were gathering speed at a break-neck pace. De-regulation had become a religion, with factory accidents on the increase and dope smuggling booming, while the factory inspectorate ran down and customs worked on a shoestring. Selling off the nation's assets to their friends became a hobby, and to many Ministers and officials a very profitable one at that. As the Government and its friends prospered, unemployment rose dramatically, maladministration was common and the fabric of the country deteriorated rapidly. It was not just a case of bad government. Their arrogance and lack of feeling gave a clear indication that they were in no way in touch with the lamentable assertion of the Chancellor that unemployment was a price worth paying in controlling inflation.

Many of my investigations centred on illegal armaments deals, the individuals involved, their contacts within the Secret Service and Government establishments and officials. I cannot and will not reveal the sources of my information, but the mechanics of

5

the 'smaller fry' are most intriguing.

You may think it strange I should mention this, but many of my 'successes', if you will pardon my attitude, followed a predictable pattern. You may have noticed that Ministers and other high officials in the nationalised industries and services, having co-operated in the sell-out to the 'privateers', or to use the modern term 'private enterprise', had decided to retire from Parliament so as to be 'with their family'. It appeared that the call of the family was irresistible and sacrificing their career, they reluctantly retired. Now don't get me wrong. They after all are human, I think? They play golf, start on their memoirs, and just as they reach the stage of settling down, the greedy devil intervenes. The privateers sail up to the threshold and the 'offer' is made. Their expertise is valuable to the private sector, would they consider an offer? The god of privatisation is hard to resist. They succumb and accept a token salary, at least tenfold of their original stipend, plus expenses, of course. And why not, when top company directors expect to survive on a 'cool million' annually? Although I despise their attitude, their arrogance never ceases to amaze me.

As an investigative journalist I was quite successful, there being a surfeit of social and political scandals just ripe for exposure. Had I been criminally inclined, I could easily have collected a million as a black-mailer. But my mother had taught me that I should treat people the way I wished them to treat me. As agreed, I forwarded the findings of my investigations to my newspaper. Even so, this was still hazardous, but to have been greedy would surely have ended in a forensic expert looking at my dead body, wondering why identification had to be so artistic.

I had just finished a stint, and now, the customs and excise having thanked me, I felt it was time for a breather. Providentially a letter from a cousin in America arrived the following morning. It was to change my mode of life for months to come. I had just finished reading the letter when the door bell rang and there he stood, the subject of the letter, all six foot three of him exuding the confidence of American football and college intelligence, 'Hello uncle,' he almost bellowed.

As he put forward his hand, I braced myself; fortunately he was a gentle giant. His grip was warm and firm, a sure indication that he wanted to be friendly. His father had told him that Uncle Wil, he was sure, would be only too willing to look after him for a fortnight while he absorbed and learned something about English jurisprudence. I was unreservedly pleased to offer my services and as rapport between us developed, he seemed genuinely interested in the opinions of a 'wise old uncle'. We spent the mornings exploring the sights of London and the afternoons inspecting and analyzing the real meaning of the sights in Parliament and what that establishment really represented. Being a bright young man, he seemed able to differentiate between truth and hot air. I did my best to entertain and guide him, spending our days hopefully in an educational fashion and our evenings in a true recreational spirit. I hasten to add that our deliberations were in no way influenced by strong drink, although both being partial to the brew of ancient monks, we did scoff a pint or two.

It was not long before I realised that my nephew was indeed a 'bright young spark'. Having majored in law, he was intent on learning the nuts and bolts of judicial systems throughout the world. He was prone to unload his findings on an uncle who, although being a provider of evidence against felons, knew precious little concerning the ramifications of the judicial system. I had to admit that much of my hard work had been wasted. My nephew had obviously done his homework before crossing my threshold. 'What is the point, uncle,' he said, 'when you have worked hard, undoubtedly taken risks, and the crook Mr X has been found guilty, sentenced to ten years in prison, is subsequently

7

found to be suffering, conveniently, from senile dementia and is released on grounds of humanity, and within months is operating as an adviser to the next generation of social degenerates?' I waved my hand and smiled indulgently towards him. Putting down his pint, he offered a tentative apology. 'I know it was a daft question but it is up to me and others of my age group to change the judicial system.' And so the evenings passed with little titbits of my experience in some of the more squalid parts of Mother Earth. The evening before he left for home he thanked me for what he considered to have been an enjoyable and interesting holiday.

In the morning I decided to deserve the day off. Having shaved and dressed, I meandered slowly downstairs to the kitchen, switched on the percolator and proceeded to the living room. I heard my mail pop through the letter box just as I drew the curtains, and there it was, the *Morning Sun*. I must hasten to assure you that I am referring to my morning newspaper, not that golden orb in the sky, so rarely seen in fog-bound London. It lay atop my mail, the headlines reading "Author Hits Jackpot". Immediately below was a picture of the author and an update concerning the popularity of his latest creation and the probability that a particular network might televise his work in the very near future. Having scanned the book during my nephew's visit, I notched it in my mind that I would read it properly at a more favourable time. As I sipped my coffee, I recollected meeting the author at a literary 'do' some years before. By the time I reached page three, I found my mind wandering a little. I was wondering what the nude model would look like if dressed in the latest fashion.

Having ensured that she was no longer topless, I was about to consider the nether region when the phone rang. It was my editor and he was in a state. The literary correspondent of the paper, Avis Ivor, had attended a wine-tasting festival. The fool had kept swallowing instead of tasting, ultimately ending up in clink, charged with being drunk and disorderly. An appointment had already been arranged to interview the author pictured on the front page and as Avis had rendered himself incommunicado, would I be good enough to fill in and save the day? As I hesitated, he lauded my performance as an investigative journalist, assuring me that my ability to emerge with honour from tricky situations would stand me in good stead.

Arming myself with the novel in question, I doubly scanned it while travelling in the tube. Collecting Avis's file, I made myself conversant with the essentials of what was in effect an adventure story, and made tracks towards the 'man of the moment'. The famous author was an old man, kind, gentle and accommodating. My assignment was to have him expound on his most recent novel. What in his estimation had made it a 'best seller' and attracted such attention from international broadcasters? I had informed him that the paper's literary correspondent had been prevented from attending the interview and as I had been seconded, I hoped he would tolerate my presence.

He smiled as he inspected my credentials, replying that he was sure no character in the novel deserved the attention of an investigator. I hastened to assure him that my function on this occasion was, hopefully, to enjoy a conversation with him regarding the most interesting parts of his novel. As far as I was concerned, it would be like a holiday and a pleasure to indulge in something creative as opposed to my daily grind of investigating the sordid affairs of corrupt politicians and devious business men, not to mention the too frequent ineptitude of the present judicial system. I knew I had overdone it as he smiled engagingly, and tut-tutting, he made me aware that none of us are angels, although it was a great pity that the majority of our society had, during the past decade, allowed the devil to obliterate too many of the hindmost. However he was sure our conversation would concentrate more on the constructive and happier side of life.

His latest creation was in a way more important to him than his successful books and plays of the past. Growing older, he felt impelled, before it was too late, to leave to posterity a little of what he had learned over the past seventy years. His novel, he hoped, could be enjoyed and contribute to man's desire to live in peace with his fellows. Although the book was a work of fiction, he admitted having his father in mind when portraying the hero and using him as a sounding board for the strengths and weaknesses of the main characters. The main character, like his father, was a Danish seaman who shortly before the first World War had settled in Scotland. Being a blithe and somewhat mercurial spirit, he made friends quickly among the Scots and as a bonus discovered that many Scandinavians had been there before him. One could describe the novel as a Scottish-Scandinavian saga or, if this offended anyone, then a Scandinavian-Scottish saga might suffice. Apart from the Scots and Scandinavians, it was an American who played an important part in the role of villain.

That afternoon the old man did me proud, insisting that if I wanted to examine the characters in any depth he would be pleased to oblige, if I was prepared to stay for an alfresco lunch. I accepted readily and enjoyed it immensely; his conception of 'alfresco' was indeed interesting and stimulating. Had I not been given my instructions to unravel some of the peculiarities of the people in his novel, I would have been quite content to expand on the author's skill in providing, on the patio, an exquisite Scandinavian smorgasbord lunch.

We discussed in a leisurely way the players in his saga and towards the end of the interview I indicated that the American, the villain of the story, was, in my estimation, an extremely interesting character. In my opinion most characters appeared real and Sorensen, the Danish sailor, although likeable as a blithe spirit, displayed the cheek of the devil at the most inopportune moments. Regarding the villain of the story, the American Ignatius Lucius Chancitt, apart from his rather ostentatious label, I found him to be malevolent but interesting.

The old author smiled as he reminded me that I was reverting to type. 'Surely,' he said, 'you should enjoy the story as such without having to investigate the seamier side of a fictional villain.' I apologised for not having the finesse of a literary correspondent, but felt that the description of the American was not just fiction. It had, despite the unlikely name, a hidden reference connected with his father in real life. The author looked at me earnestly for a full minute before confessing that his father had told him about an incident that had taken place when his ship had berthed at a South American port. His father had been approached by an unsavoury character, introducing himself as Ignatius Lucius Chancitt. He had confided, after a short spiel, that he had something to sell at an extremely attractive price. As if by magic, a small sachet of white powder had been produced. His father, realising that cocaine was being offered, had told the stranger with the queer-sounding name what he could do with his powder. A fight had developed and it appeared that he had not spared himself in flooring the dope peddlar. He remembered his father's revulsion when telling the story, the look in his eyes had remained with him; he could only suppose it had been reflected in his novel.

For a few moments there was silence. Then the old author looked at me, shook his head, then asked, 'Does the name really matter? I should have thought that being able to transmit the wickedness of dope-trafficking is far more important.' I was curious but stymied, and wondered how to react. He laughed heartily at my discomfiture and then spoke in a gentle, confidential manner. 'As far as I'm concerned, the name could well be fictitious, but that was the name the rogue offered my father, and if your curiosity has been alerted, then who am I to

11

stop you from travelling to the Americas and finding out for yourself?' Although in no way obliged to do so, he gave me all the information at his disposal and wished me 'Bon voyage'.

The editor complimented me on what he considered to have been a successful interview. I thanked him for his kind remarks, but felt somehow it was, in a way, unfinished business. For weeks I plodded on ferreting around the Whitehall warrens and scrubland, flushing out the odd 'rat' or two. It was during the time that some 'high profile' entrepreneurs were found to have been using pension funds to cover their incidental expenses.

Then one day during my bouts of depression I received an invitation from my American cousin inviting me to spend a few weeks at his fruit farm. My favourite tipple being whisky as opposed to orange juice, I put the letter on what is commonly known, these days, as the 'back burner'. A week later I changed my mind. The dampness and dreary life of Whitehall and its environs had forced me to admit that warmer climes would be more acceptable. My American cousin exhorted me to make myself comfortable and stay for at least a month.

For a week I relaxed among the orange groves, then the wander-bug bit. The face of the old author floated tantalisingly in front of me; it was as if he were exhorting me to seek out the truth. To me the names Chancitt and Chanceet seemed irrevocably linked, or was I being too subjective or romantic? I recalled that the author's father had met a dope pedlar calling himself Chancitt in a waterside tavern in Galveston, Texas. Not so far away in the Colombian hinterland there still lived, hopefully, an old man who, some seventy odd years before, had been fathered by an American known to the local peasants as Chanceet. The link could be pure coincidence, but it certainly merited close investigation and I had no intention of allowing my reputation as a 'nosy bugger' to be called into question.

However, I decided that as this appeared to be developing

into a 'busman's holiday', I would conduct the investigation in a leisurely fashion, using all the modern means of communication at my disposal. That evening I had an enjoyable conversation with my host, told him of my plans, and he, good fellow, told me to make full use of the telephone, fax, car or any modern tool that I required, and he would pick up the 'tabs'. I accepted his kind offer, and during the next two weeks I learned how to use the procedure whereby one anchors the telephone twixt ear and shoulder, leaving the hands free to write and manipulate papers while telephoning useful contacts.

At first it amused me that I was acting like some 'whizz kid' of Wall Street, but I soon realised it was saving time during the sedentary part of my investigation. Having gathered all the information I could expect from Government sources, friends in the Secret Service and social 'ad hoc' organisations, I set out first to trace the Chancitts, and secondly the probable peregrinations of one Ignatius Lucius, last seen in Galveston, Texas, and now deceased unless he had learned the secret of eternal life. My first stop was the port of Galveston, and after two days of pursuing information in official quarters I descended into the nether world, close by the wharfs. Although Scotch whisky is in my estimation the liquid 'elixir', I tolerated bourbon in the hope that it would not be too long before landing in a pub dispensing the genuine article. My luck seemed in when I landed in a tavern run by an old Irishman, who grudgingly served me Scotch but deplored my lack of education and taste. 'Surely', he said, 'the real elixir of life is Irish.'

That same day an official of the Civic Affairs Department telephoned me at my hotel. He had at my behest taken the trouble to look through the County records, and had discovered that a man named Chancitt had lived within the County boundary in the year 1880. Christian name Lord. No trace had been found concerning the area or district where he had lodged, but if I presented myself at his office I could be given a list of the County environs. Thanking him for his efforts on my behalf, I armed myself with the material he had given me and decided, at least for the present, to by-pass official sources and rely on local rumour or 'know-how'. Information could always be sought from the Pinkertons or colleagues in Washington, should the need arise.

For the next two days I cultivated the friendship of the old Irish landlord, and thought it fit, he being a Catholic, that I should confess that my education had been sorely neglected, but that in future I would only drink the true elixir, the Irish. I perused my official information in a corner adjacent to the serving point, and, as I hoped, the old Irishman spied me during a quiet spell and decided to keep me company. Three Irish whiskies later he remembered his old father telling him a story. It concerned the time when his father had been a waiter in a small township called Kerryvale, and 'sure and begorra', he had worked alongside a very temporary waiter called Chancitt, a queer customer who was English and on the run.

According to his father, it was in the eighteen-eighties that the man who had called himself Lord Chancitt served beside him for only three days before he vanished. He found out later that Chancitt had disappeared, leaving behind a great deal of debt and a pregnant maiden. The old Irishman thought that the prospect of finding anyone in the county with a name like Chancitt was indeed remote. However, as I had shown an aptitude for learning, he would if I so desired give constructive advice. As I nodded, he advised that I should travel to a small hamlet outside Kerryvale on the road leading to San Antonio.

I took the precaution of consulting maps before I set out. Too often I have been given advice when seeking a particular destination and found that we are all prone to orienteer in a haphazard fashion. I know I am. Always quick to adjust, I found I had to travel beyond San Antonio to the town of Kerryville,

14

and now know the difference between a vale and a ville. The library in the 'ville' yielded results; the young librarian pointed me in the direction concerning County Records. After a few visits to local offices and cemeteries, without results, he buttonholed me in the local hostelry. He informed me that although he was the local librarian, he lived in a small hamlet some five miles away. It was his lunch hour, and it was only fit that I should do the honours. During lunch he informed me that there was no tribe of Chancitts, but there was a record of a local spinster named Euphemia Slack who had given birth to a son, the father being an Englishman. Local gossip had it that he had been a remittance refugee from a distinguished noble family in England.

He seemed keen to clear up any mess in his own local patch, and invited me to visit his home ground, where he would be only too pleased to set the record straight. Never one to waste time, I made for the hamlet and registered at the one and only available inn. Quizzing the landlord revealed only one possible source of information. Fortunately it proved to be an excellent one. That evening after dinner as I sat in the public bar, the young librarian and a rather distinguished man entered and came straight to my table. As I rose to meet them, I knew that they had been forewarned of my presence. The young man made the introductions and I felt I was about to learn something of importance. It being my pleasure, I insisted they should indicate their favourite tongue-loosener, or whatever was required to dispel any inhibitions lounging around. Settling down with our drinks, the young man assured me that Hector Macdonald, retired lawyer and local historian, was the man best equipped to give me the information I required. He being a lawyer of Scottish extraction, I knew I would be dealing with a canny individual, who would no doubt wish to ensure that my credentials were above reproach before divulging any information that could be wrongly construed or used. After examining my credentials, he

15

admitted having read of my success in exposing and bringing to justice certain key figures in the 'cocaine scandal'.

Regarding the Chancitts, he was surprised that I was interested in a couple of rogues who at one time long ago had defiled the good name of the parish. His father had been the community lawyer before him and father, like son, had played a big part in its development. He invited me round to his practice, and I found the mass of material concerning the life of the hamlet to be extensive. Consulting his father's papers, he unearthed a copy of a letter sent to a Mr Chancitt, who, it appeared, had lodged with a spinster, Euphemia Slack. The letter had been sent on behalf of a local tradesman demanding payment of an outstanding loan of five hundred dollars. Euphemia Slack had arrived at his practice in great distress, Chancitt had disappeared, and so had her life savings. The woman was so distraught that his father had decided to handle her affairs free of charge. This was in October 1884. On July 25 1885, a child was born, and Euphemia Slack named him Ignatius Lucius, claiming he was the son of Lord Chancitt.

Being satisfied that Ignatius Lucius Chancitt existed, or had existed, I felt free to divulge the important aspects of my conversation with the old author. As the lawyer looked penetratingly at me, he said: 'To think the old devil was fictionalising a rogue from our parish and he never told me.' As I started to explain, he laughed, waved his hand indicating that it was of no account, but that he looked forward to seeing the old author in the not-too-distant future. The lawyer allowed me full scope to copy any letters or documents left in his care by Euphemia Slack, now deceased, and wished me luck in my investigations.

Taking stock, I realised I had not just set out to discover if Chancitt existed, but, if so, what type of person he had been, and what the forces were that formed his character and influenced his behaviour. The ethics and morality of the situation, just then seemed beyond me. But I was still curious and wanted to know what had happened from the time Ignatius Lucius Chancitt had left home in 1905 and probably reached Colombia some months later.

CHAPTER 2

I knew it was a tall order to follow the trail of a rogue after seventy years, but the vanity of an investigator overcame the common sense of a journalist, supposedly on holiday. Telephoning my editor, we arranged that as I would be away for some time, I would send reports on important happenings in the Americas, and that any commission earned would be forwarded to my bank account. It was not that I needed the money, but he felt it was logical I should be paid for exercising my talents on the way. It seemed only proper that I should insure myself against a rainy day; after all, I could find myself in trouble in a South American rain forest and it could be raining bullets as well as rain drops. For a brief spell such thoughts dampened my ardour, but, being stubborn, I decided to make a move. Although I knew the drill and had contacts in official circles, I knew from experience that the retention of my credentials and the goodwill of the editor would be crucial, particularly if I landed myself in trouble with the authorities. On the assumption that Chancitt had been involved in the cocaine racket, I cultivated the friendship of narcotics officers of the police and customs services of the areas through which I travelled. Also gathering material gleaned from fellow investigators and official statistics, I was able to prove that Chancitt was indeed a wicked character. I will not bore you with the details of my investigations, but can assure you that if the old author had been able to accompany me, he would have had enough material for a few more novels.

Ignatius Lucius Chancitt was the name on his passport and, though high sounding, it bore no resemblance in the least to his character or personal appearance. His lineage was essentially indeterminate. It appeared that his mother, as a maiden, had associated with a member of the English aristocracy, a certain Lord Chancitt, who as a gambler had lost everything except his title, and during a period of stress deserted his companion and joined a travelling wild-west show. Left with little money and no particular qualifications or skills, the poor maiden resorted ultimately to the practice of the oldest profession. When he was born, his mother bestowed on him the name of Chancitt in memory of her original lover. It appeared the forenames had been culled from the prophets of some mysterious religious sect to which she had belonged during her virgin years. Being a lady and a mother, she had always referred to him as her love child, but those who knew him better called him a bastard. For twenty years she fed and watered him and saw to his education, bailed him out when in trouble and went to extraordinary lengths to ensure that he would become a gentleman like his father, Lord Chancitt. It is possible that in a strange way she may have thought she succeeded. When he reached twenty-one, he demonstrated the magnanimity and politeness one would expect from a gentleman. He thanked his mother profusely for all she had accomplished. She had worked too hard for too long; he was determined to leave home and seek his fortune; she would now be free to look after herself. He joined a travelling circus just as his namesake had done many years before.

From that day on he travelled through much of America, his length of stay in any one place being determined by the time required to ensure the maximum return for the minimum effort. Often he had to travel very fast when the authorities discovered what he was up to. His nefarious activities took him up the Mississippi to Mineapolis and from Minnesota to Winnipeg in

Canada. After crossing Canada to Vancouver, he obeyed the immense hoarding urging him to 'Go West, young man'. Recognising it as a sign from the god of entrepreneurs, he set forth down the West Coast, ending ultimately in South America. His actions up to that time had been what could be termed, moderate in criminality, such as door-to-door selling of miraculous bargains, selling real estate, accepting deposits on behalf of the companies concerned and conveniently pocketing the money obtained.

It was in South America that he graduated from petty crime to the most dangerous, the dirtiest and most inhuman profession of all, that of the drug-trafficker. During his travels he had often worked as a waiter and had found this was to his advantage. It allowed him to listen in on local gossip and acquire information without exposing himself or being suspect. One day as he waited for the next victim, he became, almost accidentally, an aspiring member of the illicit drug trade. At that time he was first waiter in the notorious Taverno Amigos on the waterfront of Santa Marta in Colombia. An Englishman who had occupied a corner seat for most of the day suddenly hauled himself unsteadily to his feet and began lurching from table to table. Upsetting glasses and customers, he persisted in shouting and muttering something which, although incoherent, sounded like a warning that 'the coca plant and death are inseparable'. The Australian proprietor of Taverno Amigos was not amused and instructed his first waiter to shut that 'limey' up or toss him out. As Lucius approached, the trouble-maker managed to make his way back to his seat, where he immediately collapsed. As he lay there with his head on the table and his arms outstretched, he moaned almost inaudibly that some people were more concerned with profits than people. Ignatius looked down at the miserable drunk, contemplating the easiest way to remove him, but changed his mind when through the babbling he heard words like snow, cocaine and other slurred words that indicated the miscreant was attached in some way to cocaine trafficking.

He thought quickly, then decided that the role of Good Samaritan on this occasion could well serve his needs. For a considerable time he had been interested in what flowed from the coca plant. His interest was not botanical; more what a city gent would call the cash flow involved. During his travels through Central and South America, he had acquired sufficient knowledge to realise that the coca plant and the end product cocaine were a sure-fire winner for a man of enterprise. It was with this in mind that he sat down beside the Englishman. Putting his arm round his shoulder, he told him he was there to help. He realised at once that the man was ill and in a state bordering on terror, and if he wanted to learn anything he would have to gain his confidence rapidly; he would also have somehow to spirit him out of the tavern without arousing suspicion. While exhorting the man to trust him, he was gaining some success when he saw the proprietor approaching. He whispered in the man's ear: 'There's an Australian son of a bitch coming over and he means trouble. Now keep quiet and leave him to me.'

As Chancitt rose to his feet, the Australian bellowed, 'What the hell's going on?' Before the Australian could continue, Lucius put his finger to his mouth, waved his hand dramatically for silence, drew the proprietor away from the table and in a hushed voice explained, 'We could be in real trouble, boss, if we don't handle this drunk properly.' The Australian seemed ready to bluster but recoiled and stared wild-eyed when Lucius mentioned the word 'haemophiliac'. He was able to convince the proprietor that it would be disastrous if the man was ejected from the premises, or even left peacefully and was involved in an accident, from which he would surely bleed to death. The Australian seemed undecided but Lucius assured him he knew how to solve the problem. It was almost closing time, he could take the man home by taxi and ensure that he reached his destination safe and sound.

The Australian agreed and that was the last he saw of Lucius Chancitt and the Englishman. Taking a taxi and ensuring they were not followed, he took the man back to a room he had rented in the native quarter of Santa Marta. When the Englishman woke in the morning he was in poor shape, but although confused, he was sufficiently alert to want to know why Lucius had not taken him back to his lodgings. Mr Chancitt had everything well rehearsed. 'Listen carefully, my friend, to what I have to say. If I had taken you back to your lodgings, you would have been a dead duck by this time.' He then gave his version of what had taken place: how the Englishman, during his period of babbling, referred to Gomez who was out to kill him and Rogerson who would do the same if he did not fulfil his contract. This had alerted him to the rather menacing presence of a 'greaser' who might have been Gomez, sitting only a few tables away. As they entered the taxi, he had noticed the 'greaser' summoning a car some fifty yards away. As they neared the Englishman's lodgings, he had re-directed the taxi driver to take them to his room in the native quarter and to lose the car that was following them. He let the danger of the situation sink in before continuing. 'Let's face facts, amigo – or should I say old chap? – if you are not assassinated within the next day or two, you will most certainly die unless you are hospitalised. I suggest it is in our common interest that we should know more about each other. I am Lucius Chancitt, who are you?'

The man, in a state of shock, answered mechanically: 'I am Bill Lambert from Falmouth, England.' Lucius put an arm round Lambert's shoulders, who recoiled, feeling that the wet wing of an albatross was enveloping him. Lucius spoke soothingly. 'Let's stick together. At least we have something in common. My father was Lord Chancitt and our estate was not far from your part of the country.' Bill Lambert showed no signs of enthusiasm; he had his own views regarding the English aristocracy. This in no way deterred Lucius, who carried on regardless, outlining everything he had learned while Lambert was delirious. Lambert was almost in a state of shock when he knew Chancitt had learned so much in such a short period and realised that although hospitalisation was necessary for survival, he would not last long after the organisation found out what had happened. It was a dilemma; there had to be a solution. He felt that Chancitt, for reasons of his own, might in some way solve the problem for both of them.

Lucius seemed able to read the mind of Bill Lambert. 'Relax, Bill, I think I have a plan that could save your bacon and allow me to be compensated for my humanitarian interest in you.' He would take Lambert to hospital by taxi or ambulance, then contact the local police concerning Bill's life being in danger, and ask for a measure of protection from the people who had been threatening to kill him. Bill would supply him with the credentials he required to allow him to uplift the 'merchandise' in a place near Mompas, almost a hundred and fifty kilometres away, then travel back to a designated spot on the outskirts of Santa Marta. Here he would negotiate a deal with Rogerson which would compensate him for his effort and at the same time extract an agreement safeguarding both of them. It was decision time for Lambert. He knew he could not make the journey to Mompas and back on horseback and expect to survive. He also knew that Lucius was an acute and clever operator, who although obviously concerned with his own self-interest, had probably saved his life by whisking him away from the nightmare he had experienced in the Taverna Amigos. Knowing he was seriously ill and probably dying, he agreed to the plan, but insisted that he should go to hospital by taxi in order to allow him to stop at his lodgings and collect his personal effects and other items he might need. Lucius Chancitt smiled knowingly; the other items amused him somewhat. 'I know what you mean, my friend, just you rest while I arrange transport.'

The lodgings were in the quieter, more residential part of the town, but something unusual had happened, for instead of the normal quiet atmosphere, the place was in a state of ferment. Fire tenders, police cars, ambulances and a few hundred onlookers were clustered round what had been the big house where Lambert had stayed. It was now a burnt-out smouldering shell. Entry to the street was barred, the police official declared. Lucius was adamant. Surely something could be done to rescue what might remain of the personal effects of his friend, who was being transported in a critical condition to hospital. The officer looked sternly at the ignorant 'gringo', waved his hands in despair and curtly replied, 'Finito Senhor, see the Chief.' Lucius did just that. After dumping Bill Lambert in hospital, he told the Police Chief what had happened to his friend and how he had rescued him from the ill intention of Gomez. But it appeared he had not been able to prevent a criminal burning-down of his friend's home.

Chancitt started his journey to Mompas the next day. As he sat in the saddle, he reflected that setting fire to Lambert's lodgings while the man lay unconscious, and collecting valuable information about the cocaine organisation, had been an act of pure genius. It was more than a week later before he managed to get back to Santa Marta. Had he known the physical effort required, he might not have ventured, for Ignatius Lucius Chancitt, member of a noble family as he thought, felt that such an effort by himself was abhorrent. He did however allow himself a weary smile when he thought of the term 'donkey work', for he had found it expedient to transport the cocaine by mule. Four bags of soil, in the centre of which there nestled fifteen kilos of cocaine, a total of sixty kilos loaded on two mules had solved his transport problem.

For reasons best known to himself, he relished his next task, that of dealing with someone probably as devious as himself. Steve Rogerson, an American, was an important man in the organisation. Big, breezy and 'well met' if not well meant, he had many irons in the fire. Being an honest-to-goodness director of his own travel company in Key West and the Bahamas, he held a doctorate in agriculture. This, and membership of a prestigious association in World Health and the environment, allowed him free scope to travel the Americas with little hindrance. Despite these advantages, he was a worried man, wondering what had happened to Bill Lambert.

After two hours of kicking his heels, he decided to risk contacting the Colombian police and, in his capacity as a director of the Key West Tourist Company, he asked their help in tracing a holidaymaker who, it appeared, had lost his way. Fortunately the police were able and most willing to help. A kind gentleman named Chancitt had rescued Mr Lambert, who was a very ill man, from the clutches of a gang led by a man named Gomez. The following morning Mr Chancitt had taken Mr Lambert to hospital, knowing that he was in a critical state. Rogerson was informed at the hospital that Mr Lambert was in a state of coma and that visitors were not allowed. Three hours later, Lambert having improved, the doctor in charge allowed Rogerson in to see the patient, provided he only stayed for a few minutes. It was a frustrating experience, attempting to converse with a man who was barely alive, but he learned enough to know that a man called Chancitt would arrive some time at the rendezvous.

In the meantime Lucius had still two days of travel before he would reach the designated spot. Steve Rogerson knew he had no option but to await the coming of Mr Chancitt, trusting that he would arrive with the valuable cargo. On the third day his patience was rewarded. Lucius was sitting on an upturned box some fifty yards from a ramshackle hut that had served, in the past, as the point of contact twixt Rogerson and Lambert. Having gleaned the information that Lucius had an English aristocratic background, and being something of an anglophile, he addressed him accordingly.

'Mr Chancitt I presume?' Lucius reciprocated in similar fashion. 'You presume correctly, sir. I can only trust that you are Steve Rogerson, friend of a man called Bill Lambert.' There the pretence of good manners ended. 'Am I to assume that the merchandise is in your possession?' snapped Rogerson. Lucius was enjoying himself. 'Your presumption is indeed correct, sir, but your assumption is well off course.' Chancitt's last remark unnerved the entrepreneur somewhat. 'What d'ya mean?' he snarled. Lucius looked reproachfully at the purveyor of holidays, and advised him to 'cool it'. 'That temper of yours could lead to heart failure,' he said, and then continued, 'and waiting for your replacement could prove irksome.'

Before Rogerson could recover, Lucius looked at him fixedly and made him aware of the real facts of the situation. 'For the past week I have worked my ass off as a muleteer, transporting what you so glibly call your merchandise. I will lead you to the spot where it is hidden provided you refund the full transport cost plus the usual ten per cent of the expected profit, but first I want to see the colour of your money.'

As Chancitt leered at him, Rogerson cursed and swore, realising that facing him was a clever son of a bitch with whom he would have to bargain, also that Chancitt knew too much for his own good and that if the organisation ever found out what had happened, it could be curtains for both of them. A bargain was struck, but Rogerson, not having the 'ready', agreed that they would meet the following day. Before parting Lucius waved an admonitory finger. 'It's not that I don't trust you, Mr Rogerson, but should you have an accident or something like that, I will assume ownership of the merchandise and distribute it myself.' Rogerson laughed outright before replying. 'Look, ya bum, you wouldn't get to first base.' Lucius smiled, never a very pleasant sight, then wagging a talon-like finger at Rogerson, he warned, 'Not only do I know who all the customers and contacts are, I also know much more about the organisation you belong to than you would have dreamed possible. But if you play it straight, your gang need never know and I am sure we can work out a deal for the future that will benefit both of us.'

Rogerson was flabbergasted. He felt like killing Lucius on the spot, and as he drew breath Lucius forestalled such dastardly thoughts as he delivered the final blow. 'In case you are stupid enough to think you can have me rubbed out, I have taken the precaution of storing all I know about the organisation in a safety deposit box with instructions that it be opened if I fail to turn up two months from now. A holiday guide from your tour travel firm is also included.'

For a man used to handling people, Steve Rogerson knew he had met his match. The following day he paid up and took delivery. It was then that he was made aware of some of the vital information in the possession of the devious Mr Chancitt, knowing he would have to accept what Lucius called a plan that would work to their mutual advantage. Lucius made it clear that if he had not intervened and spirited Mr Lambert away from the Taverna Amigos, the delirious man would have blabbed to all and sundry. The Colombian Police would no doubt have been alerted and he, Rogerson, might now be languishing in jail.

Steve Rogerson was uneasy, wary and undecided, but felt he had little option but to go along with any reasonable plan that Chancitt might suggest. After all, it appeared the son of a bitch held the trump card. They agreed that Lucius would replace Lambert until the sick man recovered. Whether he did or not, Lucius made it plain that it was his intention to play his part in expanding the scope of the organisation. After all, he had contacts in the Americas and the increased business would benefit both of them.

Rogerson, feeling vulnerable, ultimately acquiesced, but there was a venomous look in his eyes as he spoke. 'For your sake it better work.' He knew that sooner or later Chancitt would have to be dumped or eliminated. But Lucius Chancitt had no illusions concerning his own safety. He knew the hazards involved but felt he would be reasonably safe until the critical period two months ahead when he might have to prove that he had planted vital information in a bank safety deposit box. The box being a figment of the imagination, Lucius was determined to maximise his profit over the next two months, and if necessary depart to pastures new considerably richer.

After four journeys between Mompas and the rendezvous on the outskirts of Santa Marta, together with some local peddling of the last consignment, he was in pocket to the tune of ten thousand dollars. He felt that despite the physical effort involved, he might at last be on to something really big. However he was brought back to earth with a thud when Rogerson informed him that after the next delivery they would both go and collect from the safety deposit the material connected with the organisation and Lambert. After all, if they were continuing their partnership, there had to be mutual trust. Lucius shivered slightly but recovered his composure and replied in accordance with a procedure he had planned some time before. 'Sure, partner, that's o.k. by me.'

As Chancitt travelled towards Mompas, he was in serious and reflective mood, wondering how far he dared go in amassing a few extra dollars without increasing the threat of immediate extinction. These tortuous reflections remained with him for the whole of the journey and the problem was still not resolved by the time he had collected the merchandise for delivery to Santa

Marta. He wandered aimlessly through the streets of Mompas, unconsciously joining a noisy but happy procession of demonstrating workers and peasants carrying banners and placards demanding land reform and increased wages. In the main they were serious but noisy. Some small groups within the procession were determined to make it more of a carnival and to some degree succeeded in causing commotion, throwing fireworks into the crowd, then attempting to pacify disgruntled spectators by offering them, gleefully, swigs from their bottles of fiery spirit.

A big brute of a man wearing an enormous hat and grinning from ear to ear encircled Lucius's shoulders firmly in a powerful arm. 'Amigo,' he belched alcoholically. It required a considerable effort from Lucius to wrench himself free, but the big man, amazingly swift despite his bulk, again encircled him and this time he was in a grip from which there was no escape. The big man laughed uproariously at the frantic struggles of Lucius. Then, lowering his head, he opened his mouth and, displaying teeth reminiscent of miniature tombstones, he asked soothingly, 'El gringo ees not happy? I take you to see Frenchie, then you happy maybe.'

Lucius gave up the struggle and relaxed, knowing there was no other option available. He felt the man did not really mean to harm him, but as he was such a strong idiot he might do so unwittingly. He conjured up a smile and, trusting to instinct, he agreed that to meet Frenchie was something he looked forward to. By the time they reached the small square in the centre of the town, the big man had quietened down considerably. Taking Lucius gently by the arm, he led him over to what might best be described as a prosperous cantina. 'This is Rosa's place,' he said. 'Now you see Frenchie.'

Lucius Chancitt felt calm. Now that there was no reason to expect immediate danger, he had enough money secreted on his person to afford some of the pleasures of life. It mattered little whether the place was a drinking den, a brothel, or both. As the big man ushered him through the door, he hopefully pictured in his mind some vivacious girl from the Folies Bergères who had, for some inexplicable reason, ended up in Colombia. He was disillusioned and mystified when introduced to a tall dark handsome man of obvious gallic charm. The big man waved his hand and announced: 'Frenchie, amigo.'

Frenchie smiled indulgently and gave the big man his instructions in a quiet cultured voice. 'You have done well, Pablo, now leave us please.' He was still contemplating the speedy disappearance of the big man as the handsome man addressed him. 'You must excuse Pablo, he knows me as "Frenchie," whereas those in our profession know me as "Snowy".' Lucius, slightly unnerved, looked sharply at the man. 'You don't mean . . ?' Before he could finish, the man opposite him smiled and replied, 'Yes I do, Mr Chancitt. I'm in the same trade as yourself.' Lucius was astounded and on edge. He knew now his position was dangerous and everything he said or did would have to be considered with great care.

Controlling his emotions, he smiled back and, in an apparently relaxed fashion, asked: 'How come you know my name and can assume that we are both in the same trade, and for that matter what is your real name and background?' The man known as Snowy was quite forthright. 'My real name is Pierre Blanc, which in English is of course Peter White. Officially I am an importer and exporter and have a particular interest in the coca plant. Over a number of years I have built up a profitable business, in the course of which I have gathered around me a set of scoundrels who have learned to do my bidding without question. I think you Americans would use the word "gang".'

He then informed Lucius that his men had been watching him for quite some time and knew that he was in some way connected with a rival gang who operated from Key West. Although still tense, Lucius could see the possibility of an arrangement, but felt he needed time to think. 'I compliment you on your choice of spies and their invisibility, but there is much more you should know, particularly about myself, and as this could take some time, I suggest we continue this conversation over drinks.' The handsome man seemed taken aback. 'Pardon my manners, monsieur, I should have ordered.' Turning his head towards the bar, he asked in a low melodious voice, 'Rosa, please.'

As they settled down with their drinks, Lucius felt that a little humbugging would not go amiss in the dense tobacco smoke and alcoholic mist. He gave a little offering. 'Monsieur Blanc, you are obviously a man of culture and breeding. I wonder if it interests you that although I was born in America, my father was Lord Chancitt, an English aristocrat who ultimately settled in Louisiana.' Snowy gave a wry smile, flicked the ash gently from the end of his cigar, took a sip of cognac then replied: 'Sounds interesting, but it may also interest you that I am a direct descendant of Le Duc Desperite, who had to make a quick exit during the revolution. However aristocratic our antecedents may have been, I fail to see how they can help us now.'

Although deflated, Lucius made a gallant attempt in the direction of sang-froid. It seemed to succeed for Snowy admitted to liking the style of Mr Chancitt, but he had to be cautious. After all, Lucius was a member of a rival organisation. Lucius knew he was in deep water and, realising the Key West gang would now surely kill him, he felt he had no option but to sell information to Snowy on the understanding that he would be protected.

As they drank together, Lucius stretched out his hand and gripping Snowy's forearm with his talon like fingers, he assured his drinking companion that he had a story to tell that would not only be interesting but would prove that he had information so vital it would mean the end of the Key West competitor and a

31

vast increase in profits for Snowy. Snowy smiled encouragingly and Lucius told the truth, the whole truth, and only omitted that which could be considered small talk. The handsome adventurer beamed at him and happily declared, 'If what you have told me is true, I could finish off the Key West gang in a couple of months.' Lucius was adamant that he was telling the truth, and expected a share in the profits that would accrue from the elimination of the Key West set-up. Also he expected protection from Snowy. Snowy smiled broadly and slapped Lucius across the back. 'If you are telling the truth, monsieur, then your life is safe in my hands and no-one from Key West will keel you, but if you are lying I will keel you.' As his knees trembled below the table, Lucius struck a dignified pose and sharply replied, 'I do not lie, Monsieur Blanc, and I know you will be man enough to apologise once your spies have done their work.' Snowy shrugged his shoulders and softly said: 'We shall see.'

It was agreed that Lucius would give sufficient information to test the validity of his assertion. In the meantime he would remain in Rosa's place until the gang returned from their foray into 'Key West' territory. Lucius Chancitt had a problem: what should he do about the consignment he had stolen from the Key West gang? If he waited too long he might have to share with Snowy's gang, or even lose the lot. But on the other hand, he could pre-empt such a situation from arising by making a deal immediately. Snowy's voice cut in on his thoughts. 'There appears to be something disturbing you, Lucius.' Chancitt did not answer at once, but kept staring into space. Then a thin smile spread over his face and he looked directly at Snowy. 'I am not disturbed,' he said, 'but I am giving deep thought to our relationship.'

He told him that although Snowy had indicated that caution had to be exercised, he felt that while verification was taking place, he was virtually in a state of limbo. This was demeaning and wasteful and particularly annoying when he could be making thousands of dollars. A certain cautious rapport seemed to be developing between the two scoundrels when Snowy asked, 'What is the problem, mon ami?' Lucius gave a good performance of exasperation as he replied: 'I have fifty kilos of cocaine stashed away, which under present circumstances I cannot unload. Like yourself, time is money and I am prepared to allow you to distribute the merchandise through your network provided you give me your word that the profits would be split fifty-fifty between ourselves.'

The French Canadian gripped his hand and shook it vigorously. The deal was solemnised with Lucius directing a parting shot at his potential partner in crime. 'At least there is now one who trusts the other.' Snowy chuckled and replied, 'Touché, Monsieur Chancitt, I trust it will not be too long before you have my apology.' Within a fortnight the two scoundrels had reached an agreement as between gentlemen.

CHAPTER 3

That they were the architects of disaster in the lives of ordinary people was no affair of theirs. They would have insisted that in the world of private enterprise, freedom of choice was the essence of democracy; in any way to inhibit or restrict it was tantamount to dictatorship. Their business grew rapidly and it was not long before they were purveying their poison in an ever-expanding market in the Americas. They grew extremely rich despite their obvious differences, or possibly because of them.

Snowy the leader of the gang was handsome and debonair, physically strong, positive in thought and definite in execution. Lucius was ugly and evil looking, his long thin arms reminiscent of some gigantic spider, moving like the arachnid in such a way that one could imagine him enveloping a weaker mortal or scurrying away to a corner at the first sight of danger, his very survival dependent on deceit and artfulness. An onlooker might have considered such a pair as incompatible but such was not the case. In the mists of time a theory or saying has evolved indicating that there is a tendency for opposites to attract. But attraction in itself is no guarantee of compatibility or a successful relationship.

That the partnership between Snowy and Lucius worked to their advantage was patently obvious, not because of some nebulous human chemistry but definitely in the way they helped each other in their business affairs. Snowy's organisation ensured the physical protection that Lucius needed and he in turn provided the stealth and cunning in spying out the land prior to the elimination of potential competitors. Also his skill in bribing and suborning government officials made smuggling that bit easier.

For two years the odd couple did well together, enjoying their ill-gotten gains, leaving behind them a trail of human disaster. Then revolution stalked the land and put a stop to their enterprise, sorely denting their aspirations for the future. With the advent of some South American governments with a leftward tendency becoming established, due to the heroic struggle of long suffering peasants and workers, great changes took place. Many of the corrupt officials the odd couple dealt with were imprisoned or executed, making life for them extremely dangerous. For a short time they held on grimly, hoping that Uncle Sam, the protector of private enterprise, would intervene and alter the political pattern of events. But it was not to be. The American cavalry did not arrive in time to save the odd couple and they in their haste had to separate and survive as best they could.

I knew I had reached a critical period in my investigations. It was obvious that the post-revolutionary governments, although marginally more progressive, had nevertheless acted as new brooms, sweeping Lucius Chancitt and Pierre le Blanc out of South America and out of business. I felt that my investigations would now have to focus in the direction of Europe. In my mind I envisaged Snowy the French Canadian making tracks for France and Chancitt travelling post haste towards England, the home of his father. Although I knew the Chancitt in the Sorenson novel was a fictional character, I felt that the real Chancitt, having already displayed certain rodent tendencies, would feel impelled to hurry 'home' and seek solace at the baronial table.

My investigations up to that point had been successful and very interesting. Even my part-time work in sending back despatches on American life had proved agreeably profitable, an indication that after six months of what I considered to be my sabbatical, I had not only increased my knowledge, but also prospered in the process. I recalled my interview with the old author some six months before. In the *Sorenson* novel, the villain Chancitt came to life in Scotland and crossed swords with the hero, the Danish seaman Sorenson. But from what source had the author been able to conjure up the character, Pierre le Blanc? Was it just pure coincidence, or did the author know that both had acted together as cocaine smugglers in South America? I could envisage my next interview with the author of *Sorenson* being very interesting.

But there was a mission of the heart to undertake. Before leaving Colombia I had decided to seek out El Chanceet, the old peasant, the bandito, who had some years before kept me alive until rescued by American agents. Had he been killed in the process? Or if still alive, where was he now? My investigations had shown Chancitt to be a womaniser of the worst type, it seemed almost certain now that Chancitt had taken advantage of an innocent Colombian maiden. Chancitt had conveniently fled the scene, and when the child was born it was natural for him to be dubbed El Chanceet. A week later I had traced Chanceet. A miraculous change had taken place since I last saw him some years before. He embraced me vigorously. I was surprised at his strength. He seemed even younger now, though in my reckoning he was nearing the end of four score years. He was no longer the poor peasant pressed into service by the coca banditos; he was now the hero of his village. From the elders I discovered that many peasants who had been pressed into banditry during the cocaine war had taken advantage of the revolution to eliminate many of the cocaine bosses and their followers. In their part of the country the coca shrubs had been destroyed and other crops had been sown in their place. There had been a showdown between the local cocaine boss and the new landowner. Sitting astride his horse and flanked by his men, the boss had issued an ultimatum. The villagers would leave the village together with their administrator and never return, or else. As he handled his pistol, Chanceet had moved the administrator aside, levelled his rifle and told the boss to defend himself. The boss had laughed but made a move and a second later he was shot from his horse. As he lay dying, the smugglers fired in the direction of Chanceet. But years of servitude had awakened in him the style of a berserker. Running in the direction of the smugglers, he kept firing and when the ammunition ran out, he grasped the barrel making ready to club; he realised then that his enemies had disappeared.

For a week I stayed in the village as a guest of Chanceet and learned all I could about the current life of the Colombian peasant, and how it compared with the time when the banditos held sway. Chanceet pointed to two pieces of armament in the far corner. To me they looked like sten guns. For a moment he was sad, then he admitted that life could be better. The peasant government was still too undecided as to how it should deal with the cocaine cartel. But one thing was certain. If the banditos returned they would be killed. Every villager was armed; they were not inclined to rely on the government intervening in a positive way.

One old man of ninety recollected the arrival in the village of an American who was supposedly an expert on the coca shrub. He became known as the 'coca man' or Mr Chancitt, the name of the absconding American. The villagers had tolerated his presence, believing him to be an agronomist who might help the rural economy. He had stayed awhile with a young maiden who had no family ties. Their suspicions had been aroused when he mysteriously vanished during a raid by government troops seeking cocaine smugglers. Some months later they were enraged when they discovered the 'coca man' had defiled the young maiden, leaving her with a burden. The progeny, a son, had been named El Chanceet, this being similar to the name of the absconding American rascal. The ninety year-old man described El Chanceet as a small ugly child who, unfortunately, at a young age had all the characteristics of his father, but with one exception: his eyes were the eyes of his mother. Although saddled with the name 'El Chanceet' and referred to as the bastard of an American 'gringo', he had tolerated insults and bullying in silence. He was the exact opposite of his brash, cruel and devious father. He could be described as a type of stoic, displaying little emotion when harassed, which was often when he was young, accepting praise graciously but almost passively after performing some good deed on behalf of his fellow men.

During the revolution the villagers had thought fit to arm themselves. The village elder had offered a rifle to Chanceet but he had refused to take it and had only accepted it after being told that he, the elder, would never forgive himself knowing that he had not done his duty in providing him with a means of defence. I was about to question this when the elder intervened. Putting a finger to his lips, he asked me to be patient, and then told me a story.

'Some years ago during the cocaine wars, when our village was in the front line, it was difficult to tell friend from foe. Our position at that time can best be summed up by the American saying, "Are you for the company or the union?". Our village was for unity against the power of the exalted cocaine barons. In such a battle the rich and powerful often subvert the poor and vulnerable. The issue was also complicated by the intervention of freebooters like Lucius Chancitt and American secret service agents. Our village leader had, unknown to us, transferred his allegiance to the cocaine bosses. Many of us, including Chanceet, had been pressed to protect, as we thought, the "local economy". During that period Chanceet worked incessantly to overthrow the power of evil, but even then I cannot remember him using the rifle except when he shot the man who threatened us, and

38

even then it was to defend an unarmed man.'

As the old man hesitated I smiled, recollecting the time when, as a prisoner, Chanceet had sat opposite me, a rifle resting across his knees. The old man read my mind. 'You were fortunate, my friend, I saw you when you were our prisoner. Chanceet was chosen to guard you; he would not have killed you or allowed others to kill you. He is a remarkable man, and like the Indian, can read the signs for many miles around. He had a premonition of movement before the Americans attacked and had already fastened a white sheet of surrender to the door of your prison, retiring to a position where he could overlook and intervene if he saw fit.'

The whole of the last day in the area was spent in the presence of Chanceet. He was still curious, wishing to know as much as he could about life beyond the borders of Colombia. On the last occasion his questions to me had been rather negative, wondering if in other parts of the world the people suffered to the same degree as the peasants of Colombia. This time he was more constructive and enthusiastic, wishing to be made aware of conditions and practices that could advance the standard and quality of life in his own village. I did my best despite my limited knowledge of the Spanish and Portuguese languages, and left him the addresses of some liberal and socialist organs in South America. As I tried to understand and help him in his deliberations, he looked searchingly at me.

His gaze was at first gentle; there was a luminosity in his eyes akin to that of a dark-skinned child. But as he strove for truth, the strength of character of the real man shone through, sending a clear message that to achieve his aim he could tolerate no evil from within himself or in others. We talked well into the evening and as darkness fell and our discussion ended, he enveloped me in his lean but powerful arms and thanked me for my patience and understanding. When I told him about my mission, he was enthusiastic and wished me well, hoping that some time in the near future I would return. 'After all,' he said, 'our companionship is something special.'

My send-off in the morning was something I had not anticipated. Chanceet had lined up the elders of the village to cheer me on my way. As they wished me 'bon voyage' in their own way, I posed one last question to Chanceet. 'Tell me, my friend, do you know the date of the day you were born?' He asked me for paper and pencil and as he wrote, he smiled and suggested that an honest man deserved the truth. Once more on the trail of Lucius Chancitt, I struck southwards, feeling that he would have wished to distance himself during an awkward period from the attentions of Uncle Sam's Narcotics Department. For an investigative journalist this was of course sheer guesswork, considering it was now some eighty years since he had practised his rotten trade in that part of the world.

Armed with information obtained from Chanceet and the village elder, I started southwards. After a week of questioning old people in villages and farmsteads en route, I satisfied myself that he had been seen in the area many years before. They remembered him as a transitory but grotesque figure, who resembled a black-coated spider with the hooked nose of a vulture. For a brief period he had accompanied a well-known bandit of French origin, known as Pierre.

After leaving Colombia the trail ran cold, and for another three weeks of dilly-dallying and sometimes exposing myself to unnecessary danger in South America, I decided to rely for information on the Narcotics Departments of the various republics. It was in Uruguay that something tangible surfaced. It appeared to me that Lucius, using his money and guile, had ultimately reached Montevideo. From the customs in that port I discovered that after manoeuvring and haggling, he had managed to book a passage to Italy. My first impulse was to contact some of my journalist friends in Europe to trace the movements of Mr Chancitt. Almost immediately I knew I would be wasting their time and my own, in view of the time lag of more than seventy years.

As a European investigation could take longer than I wished, I thought it sensible to indulge myself before proceeding further. In any case I am not particularly fond of Italian food. Knowing I would receive a welcome back from my American cousin, I boarded the first available ship travelling in his direction. As it made its slow journey towards Galveston, I thought of Hector Macdonald, the lawyer in the small hamlet near Kerryville. A few days spent in that area appealed to me. As a refresher it could prove enjoyable and rewarding and, after all, the orange groves were not too far away. I found that Hector's curiosity had been aroused since my visit and he had taken the time and trouble to delve into the papers of his lawyer father. It appeared that Lucius Chancitt, apart from reneging on a five hundred dollar loan, had also managed to part a well-known politician from a sum of two thousand dollars.

Macdonald senior, knowing he had political backing, used the register of malingerers and remittance opportunists who had been plaguing the erstwhile colony for longer than could decently be tolerated. Through diplomatic channels the address of the Chancitt family had been obtained. There was no guarantee that the letter sent to England had been received, or that the address was indeed genuine, but if I wanted to pursue the matter further the address was available. The address was definitely noted.

Hector showed me a copy of the letter sent to the head of the Chancitt family warning him that the family escutcheon was in peril of being soiled, and asking that he accept responsibility for honouring the debt and disciplining his wayward offspring. I stayed with Hector Macdonald for two nights, and during that time I learned that his association with the old author had been considerably more than just a transitory meeting of scribblers. It appeared the author had started life as an apprentice in the Engineering Faculty of Edinburgh University, giving him an insight into student and proletarian life. Qualifying as an engineer, it was not long before he became involved in union affairs. Within months he had been elected shop stewards' convener in a factory connected with the Admiralty. It being war time, certain sly employers often with the assistance of the secret service, used the Defence of the Realm Act for their own nefarious purposes. A militant shop steward organising and fighting on behalf of his fellow workers could expect the establishment to have him incarcerated as a potential spy. The author had received such attention, and although he was not imprisoned, he was awarded the dubious honour of an interview by two men from the local CID. These, acting on instructions from the secret service, had failed miserably to make his life uncomfortable. It had angered him that two honest policemen had been misused for such a purpose by either MI5, MI6, or some other sneaky adjunct of Government dirty tricks.

When the war ended and 'pay offs' were in fashion, he was sacked along with two hundred of his mates, the militant ones of course. To show there was no ill feeling, he was given a glowing testimonial by his employers for his outstanding efforts during war time. He found, however, his reference must have been coded, for the wee black ball kept rolling and doors kept slamming in his face as if operated by remote control. From then on he had operated on his own, accepting his inability to change dramatically man's selfish attitude to his fellow man.

Forced to leave the industrial field, he survived as a salesman, sales manager and then qualified as a physiotherapist. It was at this point that Hector stopped for a breather and excusing himself, walked over to his library and returned with several books. Laying them down in front of me he asked if I was conversant with the works of the American author, Upton Sinclair. Assuring him I had read the books of Upton Sinclair, I emphasised that I also believed in the socialist programme he espoused. He smiled at my reaction.

'At least,' he said, 'there are three of us who believe that the acceptance of social principles could alleviate a great deal of human suffering in this selfish world of ours.' He ended his story by telling me that the author of *Sorenson* had decided that as his agitation and organising of the working class was becoming less than cost effective, he felt he had no option but to substitute brain for brawn. Realising that entertainment provided a platform for progressive thinking, he had decided to use his talents in that direction. It had been an uphill struggle. After all his only literary work up to that point had been the production of a *Workers' Bulletin*, appearing weekly and costing a penny. It had definitely contributed to an improvement in working conditions and wages. It was frowned upon by tight-fisted employers and certain government officials, particularly the Home Office, this despite the editor agreeing with Churchill that 'our glorious allies', the Soviets, were tearing the guts out of the German war machine.

But during peacetime a different strategy was called for in what he recognised as the class war. He had admitted to Hector that changing his mode of life from one of physical activity to what he called his sedentary vocation had been difficult, but considered it in the end most rewarding. Having found a publisher prepared to accept his material, he had been successful with two novels. Both had been light reading, comedy and sarcasm being the main ingredients, with the establishment being mercilessly lampooned.

Suddenly Hector changed the subject. Whether he thought he was boring me or had reached a stage privy to the author and himself, I will never know. 'Mr Ling,' he said. 'I've done most of the talking so far. I would deem it an honour if you would put me in the picture concerning the experiences and hazards one can expect as an investigative journalist.' I repaid his contribution towards the Chancitt investigation by telling all that I had learned and experienced from the beginning up to the time I had met him, also what I had learned since. By one in the morning, conversation had slowed somewhat and by mutual agreement we decided that a pleasant end to an interesting and delightful evening was called for. He raised his glass to me. 'I wish you success,' he said, 'in all your endeavours.'

CHAPTER 4

Next morning, armed with the address and some facts concerning the background of the aristocratic family of Chancitt, I travelled post haste to the warmer climes of Florida. Being fond of sea travel, I had originally thought of crossing the Gulf of Mexico, but changed my mind, deciding that the flight to Tampa would prove cheaper, a good deal faster and possibly more interesting. On reaching Tampa I headed for Clermont, having heard of the Citrus Tower and the view of the orange groves that covered the landscape. What I saw was disappointing. From where I stood to as far as I could see, there were only gnarled and dead-looking trees. There may have been oranges around, but they did not advertise their presence. I was to learn later that the whole of the State's orange crop had been wiped out in the big freeze of 1985.

As I made my way northwards to the Ocala and Silver Springs area, I wondered how the big freeze had affected my cousin. I remembered my mother telling me about her family, the Munros. How as original settlers they had survived the Seminole Indian wars, and had prospered as cattle raisers despite raids, the infrequent but damaging freeze, and the all too frequent hurricanes. It was with a slight feeling of trepidation that I arrived at the homestead of Neal Munro. The main building, a two-storied Victorian house of good design and in good repair, was a pleasure to the eye. But the sight of orange trees on either side of the approach path surprised me, considering what I had been told at the Citrus Tower.

I had little time to speculate for a young giant was approaching me. He shook my hand and pumped it vigorously in friendly fashion, while I attempted to absorb the shock. 'Welcome, Uncle,' he said, 'Dad will be pleased to see you.' Suddenly I realised I was in a different house. The young prospective lawyer must have seen the perplexed look on my face for he immediately enquired what was on my mind. When I told him, he explained that the last time we had met, it had been at Orlando Airport and from there he had driven me to the old fruit farm some thirty miles away. My mistake had been to tell the driver of the limousine to take me to the 'Munro place'. It appeared that I had been taken to the fruit farm on the first occasion, the original settlement of the Munros some two centuries before. Since then the Munros had expanded their holdings, alternating between fruit and cattle. The rolling hills, the lush meadows and the fresh water springs had proved ideal for raising cattle and horses. Although the fruit farm had been retained as a halfway house between the ranch and the Orlando Business Center, it was no longer recognised by the locals as the 'Munro Place'. However his father still had a soft spot for the original settlement and conducted much of his business from there. Having already spent two weeks at the fruit farm and enjoyed it, I wondered why the Munro family preferred staying at what was now known as the 'Munros'.

Although born in Florida, Neal Munro still displayed the characteristics of the Scot, shrewd, canny and kind enough to answer questions in his own pawky fashion. That evening, between sips of Old Antiquary and fresh spring water, he gave me what amounted to a short history lesson. The Munros and other Scots who settled in Florida had established cattle ranges, and some, influenced by Greeks and Italians, had found the citrus trade more profitable. His eyes twinkled as he informed me that

46

to the best of his knowledge the first Munro started as an orange grower in the area now known as the fruit farm, the place where I had first met him. Being a Scot, he wished to be as accurate as he could.

'I have proof,' he said 'that Neal Munro, a namesake of mine, had orange groves over two hundred years ago in the vicinity of the fruit farm.' As I nodded, appreciating his desire to ensure my education was brought up to date, he continued: 'But I should make allowance for three members of the Munro clan who left Inverness some fifty years before my namesake with the intention of reaching America. Whether they ever settled in Florida I cannot tell you, but you, Mr Ling, having a Munro mother, might be able to tell me?' I assured him my mother had indeed made me aware of the enterprising spirit of the Munros; my knowledge however was limited and certainly not as extensive as his. But I was interested and willing to learn of the exploits of my mother's 'ain folk'. He toasted me in good spirit and could not resist a pawky remark. 'I know you are interested, and that is as it should be; after all, you are Wil Ling'.

I was to learn that the original Munro and my cousin had both been imbued with the pioneering spirit and had trodden similar paths. Although both had started on the 'citrus road', freak storms and the odd frost or two had dictated diversification. Neal, like his forefathers, had recognised that the conditions were ideal for raising horses and cattle. There was also the added bonus of good fishing in clear unpolluted water. From the start the Munros had established good relations with the Seminole Indians, learning from their ancient wisdom the most effective way of combating the vagaries of the weather and its effect on the land. Seminole 'know-how' and Scottish sagacity had evolved the policy of diversification, so that if and when the odd frost damaged the orange groves, their cattle farms and horse ranches more than balanced their 'citrus deficit'.

With millions of Americans and Europeans flocking to sunny Florida for the 'holiday of a lifetime,' he felt he had a duty to make the tourists aware of the advantages of holidaying in central Florida. There was more to a holiday than just acquiring a suntan on the man-made beaches of Miami. A tan could still be acquired in central Florida, a land of streams, sparkling springs, clear rivers and lakes. After all, the same sun shone in central Florida, and the razzle-dazzle of Miami was not essential for every tourist. According to Neal, the 'Munros' was the ideal holiday place for those tourists who enjoyed and admired natural beauty. The discerning tourist, the sportsman, and the 'oldsters' who preferred the pleasure of leisure were all catered for. Neal stressed that the Munro place was near the National Ocala Forest and for those interested in golf, the Golden Ocala golf course was not far away. He became quite effusive.

'You know, Wil, I'm an extremely fortunate man. What with the oranges blooming again, thousands of cattle in good fettle and more than a thousand thoroughbred horses raring to go, I must be the richest man in central Florida, and yet I have this yen to visit the old country.' As I agreed with his sentiments, he continued. 'Having control over so much, I feel like a Scottish laird, but I know I have as much respect, if not more, from my tenants and tourists, and what's more I can enjoy it in a warmer climate. But who knows? One day I might just visit my roots.'

Having read Fodor's *Florida*, I felt I had to make some contribution. I admitted to having read about Florida in an off-hand fashion, but remembered that the green pastures of the Ocala region were ideal for the rearing of horses, and the land between Ocala and Inverness was a paradise for thoroughbreds. For a moment I paused, wondering if the mention of Inverness struck a chord. Neal Munro laughed heartily, and putting his hand on my shoulder, he asked to be allowed to speak. As I nodded he said, 'I think you were wondering if the three Munros who left

Scotland for the Americas some two hundred and fifty years ago may have settled nearby and named the place after the capital of the Scottish Highlands.' As I admitted to that possibility, he assured me he had already asked the various authorities and so far the answer had been in the negative. Turning to his son, he asked for his opinion.

'Do you think that Wil, being an investigative journalist, could maybe solve the mystery of the three rascals who disappeared so long ago?' Neal junior was quick to reply. 'As a lawyer I would say the possibility of establishing the modus operandi and ultimate destination of three persons who vanished two hundred and fifty years ago is extremely remote. After all, Uncle Wil is finding it difficult enough to find out what a certain cocaine smuggler was doing approximately a century ago.' I looked fondly in his direction before replying. 'Your son is right, Neal, it could take some time. For that matter, the crossing of the Atlantic in the first half of the eighteenth century was still hazardous and unpredictable.' I hesitated and, with my tongue in my cheek, I offered to do my best to discover what had happened to three of his kin. Neal shook his head and replied, 'Deed no, I would not want you to waste your time. From what I have learned, they were scallywags anyway.' Taking advantage of his generosity and the remarks of his son, I asked him a favour. 'Could I spend a few days at the fruit farm and make use of the facilities?'

He agreed readily but seemed amused and asked what was so special about the fruit farm. When I told him that I wished to pursue the Chancitt case a little further, he burst out laughing. 'Stay here and enjoy yourself, Wil. The fruit farm is only my half-way house; there are far more tools of your trade here than up at the fruit farm.' Neal junior supported his father, telling me that the Munro place was equipped with telephones, faxing equipment and an up-to-date computer system; everything I would require was on hand. Neal Munro thought fit to butt in: 'Give junior a brief of what you require and let me take you on a tour of Florida.'

Junior seemed quite excited and agreed that I should brief him on what was required. He hastened to assure me that as a lawyer he had many contacts, knew the type of questions to ask, and that after all he had learned a few wrinkles from me during his holiday. 'Enjoy yourself, Uncle,' he said, 'see Florida and let me do the sleuthing.'

Holidaying in Florida had never been on my agenda, although some years ago I had had occasion to visit Miami in connection with a vice scandal involving certain members of so-called high society. I realised at that time that apart from vice, Florida had a lot to offer the sun and fun seekers of the world. As a tourist I would have wanted something more; the hard sell of the holiday brochure or agent was not endearing to me despite the beauty of that sun-drenched sandy strip of land. Although not overly keen, I was pleasantly surprised to learn that it was his intention to avoid the sun beaches on the Atlantic side and concentrate on exploring central Florida. I accepted his kind offer, feeling it would have been churlish to do otherwise, and he smilingly assured me that it would be interesting.

As we left the ranch the following day in a rather high-sided Range Rover, Neal junior thought fit to put me at ease in an expanded version of the normal American greeting. 'Have a nice fortnight, Uncle,' he said. 'I'll have a load of information for you when you return.' My glance at him must have been of the enquiring type, for he thought fit to assure me cheerily, 'No problem.' I'd heard that before but accepted it in the true spirit of fellowship, knowing I would be capable of making adjustments if required.

We headed north through country known as the 'big scrub'. On my map it indicated that we were now in the region designated as the Ocala National Forest. It was just as Neal had described it, forests of hardwood trees, the clean clear water of

50

the springs, the rivers, the lakes and the rolling hills, ideal for the rearing of thoroughbred horses. Much of the floor of the Ocala forest consisted of sand and the close-packed trees were appropriately named sand pines. Having always associated the word scrub with the utensil brush, I wondered if the word scrub referred to the action required to clean up the brushwood embedded in the sand. As I offered my opinion, my companion smiled indulgently, assuring me I was on the right track, unlike the greenhorn from New York who thought that scrub or brush wood was wood used in the manufacture of scrubbing brushes.

Anxious to further my education, Neal pointed to isolated sand dunes on which grew prickly vegetation. Starting with the rather ingenuous 'Once upon a time,' he continued, 'many thousands of years ago Florida was a desert, much the same as the Sahara and other deserts known to man, its topography being determined by winds and tides.' My curiosity aroused, I asked Neal if I could walk a part of the Floridian scrub land. He seemed amused but readily agreed.

As we walked, I felt my feet sink deep into the sand. Even with my shoes on I could feel the rapid increase in temperature, and had to admit that although I was not a New York greenhorn, I did feel like a British tenderfoot. Slapping me on the back, he assured me I was learning fast. He was sure I would enjoy the experience and his remark, 'You ain't seen nothing yet,' was not encouraging. To be honest, I had to modify his assurance that I learned fast and substitute for it the much used cliché, 'It was a most interesting experience.' Apart from the rattlesnakes I almost stepped on, I did manage a nervous smile as little red spiders skated over my boots, and managed to look calm despite lizards jumping in front of me from nowhere.

Back in the car, Neal expounded the views of the experts, who would have it that the first vegetation on high ground was sparse and scraggy. Over many thousands of years hurricanes and torrential rain had shaped the sand dunes. The scrub's water supply had been sparse and transient, while the great mass of water had seeped down to the water table in the hard core of the earth's surface, subsequently giving greater nourishment to vegetation at the lower level.

The bigger terraces of sand formed what was now described as the 'Highlands of Florida'. Those dunes stretched from north of Ocala to Lake Okeechobee. As we travelled north through lush pastures and effervescent springs, I saw from time to time the odd bit of scrubland cropping up, as if to say, 'I was here first.' Neal felt it important that I should know that at one time the scrub covered much of Florida and that he and many others had become prosperous orange growers after clearing the land and ensuring it got its fair share of rain. As I pondered the mechanics of an equitable distribution of water, my companion shook his head and feigning a look of despair, murmured rather loudly, 'Well, well, Wil.'

I recovered in time to tell him I was not the complete tenderfoot; my mind had been absorbed by the beautiful scenery, and therefore the artistic had temporarily taken precedence over the artesian. Neal laughed heartily, agreeing that my remarks were indeed apt, and felt it necessary to inform me that although a man of the soil, he did appreciate my type of repartee. I assured him that normally I was not considered to be a witty person, but on the odd occasion, as an investigative journalist, I had to be quick witted to get myself out of trouble.

By the end of the day we knew each other well, Neal acting as teacher and host, and I as the pupil and privileged visitor. We struck westwards towards the Gulf of Mexico and stopped in the evening at Cedar Keys. We dined at the Maison Miraculous, a most unusual restaurant. The front of the building overhung the sea and was supported on stilts. The main dining hall had big french windows opening out to a balcony overlooking the harbour. My companion ushered me out to the balcony and as we sat down he told me that Cedar Keys was renowned for sea food, and in his opinion the Maison Miraculous topped the lot. It appeared that Miki Miraculous, a Greek fisherman, had married Collette, the proprietress of a small Parisian restaurant. The skills of both, according to Neal, were manifested in the finest devilled crab in Florida and possibly the world. I cannot claim to be an expert on sea food, but I can say that the devilled crab was rather exceptional and why not? It was called 'Crab Miraculous'.

As we finished our excellent meal, our host came to our table and asked if we would kindly remain seated, relax, and he would tell us a story. As Neal laughingly assented, he stretched his arms out to the limit, making a proviso that it was not about the one that got away. Miki waved his arm aside in a contemptuous fashion and although I had difficulty following his Greek American brand of English, I realised that he was indicating that as a fisherman all his life, amateur angling had never appealed to him as a hobby. He had fished in the Black Sea, the Aegean and the Mediterranean. Latterly he had acquired his own boat and concentrated on fishing among the islands of the Ionian Sea. Twixt shrimp fishing and smuggling, he had enjoyed a peaceful and profitable lifestyle. He had become a respected member of Corfu society, mainly through his generous donations to the fund for distressed fishermen and their families.

Despite my difficulty in understanding him, I knew by Neal's reactions that he considered him a good man, and that was good enough for me. He concentrated on the crustaceans of the sea and in the main on shrimps; it was these small decapods that had made him a rich man. Despite difficulty in following his narration, I was quite content to listen to his deep melodious voice. As the tempo increased, I knew he was working towards a climax. Suddenly he stopped, and as his eyes shone, a grin spread slowly while his arm rose and his finger pointed to the horizon.

For almost a minute he said nothing, then gracefully lowering his arm he pointed in the direction of the harbour entrance. For some seconds we saw only the sinking sun and, as he gave a little gurgle of delight, the leading boat of the shrimping fleet entered the harbour. Turning to us, his eyes shining, he asked, 'Is it not a beautiful sight? Something, I'm sure, that would gladden the hearts of most men.'

There could be little doubt that anyone who witnessed the shrimp fleet coming into the harbour, with the slanting rays of the setting sun throwing into relief those colourful craft as they glided majestically to their moorings, would be bound to agree and rejoice. But before we could answer Miki, a female voice disturbed our reverie. It was the voice of a contralto, and it issued from the lips of a beautiful woman, who could best be described as a well-proportioned svelte lady with an acute sense of humour. 'Pardon me, Messieurs, but I cannot allow my husband to act like Chauvin and forget that women's hearts are also gladdened when their menfolk return from the sea.'

Miki was equal to the occasion. Rising from his seat, he introduced us to his wife Collette. Having ensured that she was sitting comfortably, he apologised. 'Had I known that you were in the vicinity, Collette, I would most certainly have included the women in my statement. I can only apologise, but would add that it hurts me grievously that you should compare me, a handsome and romantic Greek sailor, with that ridiculous misfit French soldier.'

Her controlled laughter was a delightful experience. Her sensuous willowy frame seemed to expand as the round of merriment circled its way upwards to a joyous crescendo. Then, breathing deeply, she shook her head and relaxed before replying. 'Just not good enough Miki,' she said, 'you are romantic when it suits, but I'm sure your heart is more gladdened when your three boats come home heavily laden with shrimp.' Miki looked at us, raised his arms sideways with palms towards us, and, accepting defeat, he could only whisper loudly, 'What can I say, Messieurs?'

That was the start of some witty banter between husband and wife, reflecting a rapport designed to amuse and entertain themselves and very special friends. Knowing that Neal belonged to that category, I felt it an honour that I was being considered in the same fashion. They begged us to stay the night in their special guest bedrooms facing out to the Gulf of Mexico, but first we would accept drinks while we conversed and supper before we retired. It had been five years since Neal's last visit and, as might have been expected, many changes had taken place. Fortunately the upturn in tourism had helped both Neal and Miki. Sea food and boat trips were high on the agenda these days. For Neal, polo and racing had increased the demand for thoroughbred horses, the cattle trade had increased, even the orange crop had given a sweet return.

It was towards the end of the evening before Neal and my new-found friends exhorted me to unload some of my experiences. Having heard I was an investigative journalist, Miki and Collette were very curious. Although I was to regret Collette's immediate reaction, I saw no reason for not telling about my investigation into the life of Lucius Chancitt. No sooner had I mentioned his name than Collette almost shouted: 'Who did you say?' She quietened a little when I stressed that the man I was investigating was probably dead. Nodding agreement but still very disturbed, she asked to be allowed to tell a story concerning a man of the same name.

Collette recalled her mother telling her when she had reached a certain stage, how her virginity and self-esteem could be threatened unless she knew how to handle the attentions of men. It appeared that Collette's grandmother, when only nineteen, had, together with a friend, set out early one evening to have a peek at life in a notorious district of Paris. What they did see shocked them, but it did not deter them from entering a street café and ordering coffee. As they sipped their coffee, two men entered and came over to their table. They were an odd couple, the first man was tall, handsome and pleasant, the other thin and cadaverous with a constant leer for a face. The handsome man politely tipped his hat and asked if they might be allowed to share their table. The young women, inexperienced in such matters, diffidently agreed. Little did they know that their curiosity would end in tragedy.

Collette sighed softly, took a sip of her drink and then continued. Her grandmother had been alerted when the men suggested they accept a drink. With coffee still in their cups, the two women rose from their table and, declaring they would be back shortly, left the café surreptitiously, hoping they had not been seen. As they made their way homewards they laughed nervously, wondering what might have happened. Once clear of the district, they decided on their next rendezvous and then made their separate ways home.

In the morning the local newspaper focussed attention on a horrendous event that had taken place in a small woodland not far from her grandmother's home. The dead body of a young woman had been found. She had been raped and then strangled. When her grandmother discovered that it was her friend who had been killed, she wept solidly for two days, blaming herself for what had happened. On the third day, having recovered her composure, she approached the police and informed them what had happened on that fateful evening.

The officials, being concerned with facts, asked her to be as objective as possible, knowing that in her present emotional state valuable clues could be missed. Although they had been in the company of the men for only a few minutes, had any names been mentioned? She recollected that the ugly one had referred to his companion as Pierre, and he in return had replied with what appeared to be a female name like Lucy. After describing to the best of her ability the physical characteristics of both men, she was thanked for her assistance.

For two months she fretted and undertook detective work that could easily have ended in a similar tragedy. Just as she thought her efforts would never bear fruit, she was called before the District Magistrate and asked to identify the man she had suggested might have been called Lucy. She replied that he was the man and that he had accompanied the tall man whom he had referred to as Pierre. After identification, she was taken aside by the Magistrate for further questioning and discovered that the man with the leering face was known as Lucius Chancitt, an American adventurer and cocaine smuggler. Already remanded in custody on a charge of illicit drug dealing, he was now likely to be charged with murder.

Three months later, just prior to his trial for murder, the man known as Lucius Chancitt escaped. At that point Collette stopped and, looking at Neal and me, shook her head sadly and concluded. 'I'm sure,' she said, 'the American called Lucius Chancitt killed my grandmother's friend that night. I do know that my grandmother never forgave herself, and never forgot to the day she died. I know now that man Chancitt is probably dead; may he burn in hell eternally.'

There was a deathly silence. Then Miki saw fit to enjoin his friends to be happy; he saw no point in allowing the incineration of a felon to interfere with their jollity. For a fleeting moment Collette looked angrily at her husband and was about to reply. But he, still smiling, gripped her arm firmly, indicating his advice applied to her even more. She softened visibly, then placing her hand on his, she agreed that the dead should not be allowed to interfere in the festivities of the present.

CHAPTER 5

From Cedar Keys we travelled down the West Coast in the direction of the Everglades and that ultimate tail end of America, Key West. Four days later we arrived at Tampa. It had been a leisurely trip, my companion seeing to it that I was well briefed during the journey. Each evening, wherever we stopped, Neal ensured that we enjoyed the company of friends. The social round had been enjoyable, but nothing quite so poignant as the evening at Maison Miraculous. I felt now I should never have mentioned the name Chancitt in the presence of Collette, but it had been done, proving that whether he had killed the girl or not, he was as I suspected, a womaniser of the worst type.

Although pleasantly absorbed in the holiday, I was beginning to wonder how much of the Sorenson novel was really fictional. I could not recollect the author telling me that he knew of a partnership between Chancitt and Pierre. However, to me the present was more important than a ghost of the past and, being in a happy mood, I concentrated on the future. It is unlikely I will ever forget my short sojourn in the Tampa area. We had lodged for two nights in a Greek hotel owned by friends of Neal and Miki. Knowing Neal's background, he had advised us to visit Dunedin, a small town between Tarpon Springs and Tampa. With the time factor in mind, Neal hummed and hawed for a few moments and then our host, a Greek, surprised us by exhorting Neal in a familiar tongue.

'Dinna waste time, dae it the noo,' he said, a big grin spreading over his face. Neal took him at his word and we set out immediately for Dunedin. As we travelled, I asked Neal laughingly why the Greek had used the Scot's language. He told me it was not all that unusual and explained that Scots and Greeks together had frequented that area probably over the last three centuries and would know a great deal of each other's customs, culture and language. There was a smile on his face as he assured me that the word Dunedin was Gaelic, an indication that the Scots had been in the ascendancy when the town was named. The wailing of the bagpipes proved his point, for we had arrived just in time to enjoy the annual Highland Games. As a young man I had been fairly competent in various sports and, knowing the effort required, I have always enjoyed any spectacle where speed, strength and agility are demonstrated; if poetry in motion be added, it makes my day.

Regarding the musical part of the programme, I could not make an expert analysis, but I did enjoy the agility displayed by the terpsichorean toddlers, who, in their Highland dress, flung themselves exuberantly into the dance. I'm sure if my attitude had been in the negative, their mothers would soon have made me aware of my ignorance and lack of feeling. Having witnessed a number of Highland Games in Scotland, I looked forward to the heavy events. Whether it was the time scale or the growth factor in the developed world, I could not be sure, but one thing was certain: the athletes looked bigger and stronger. I was in no position to judge whether the American Scot had overtaken the homebred athlete, but was well satisfied to see a seventeen stone man throw, one-handed, a fifty-six-pound ring weight up and well over a bar seventeen feet from the ground. Neal told me some time afterwards that the man's name was Mackenzie and his mother was Grecian. Had I known that at the time, I might have visualised a young Greek athlete invoking support from the appropriate god as the weight flew heavenwards.

After our Highland fling, things became more nautical by the mile. In my mind I saw Tampa not so much as an airport; more as a gateway to the waterways of the South West Coast of Florida. Having already seen Tarpon Springs, we headed for St Petersburg and its numerous beaches. It was to be the start of motoring bridges and causeways. There were times when, the further south we travelled, the more water there seemed to be as compared with land. Passing a causeway aptly named Sunshine Skyway, we crossed a newly-built suspension bridge which led to scenic views of Tampa Bay. Tampa being a very busy port, I paid scant attention to the deep-sea freighters, the shrimpers and other commercial craft and concentrated my mind on the small islands dotting the seascape. After all, I am acquainted with many of man's errors as he pollutes his own environment and therefore take every opportunity to enjoy the beauty of nature wherever I find it. For the true artist the West Coast of Florida must be heaven indeed. My first view of the seascape and the glorious sunset at Cedar Keys was repeated many times at the places we stopped on our way southwards. But I will not forget the ultimate experience at Key West. I had already been told what to expect and I was not disappointed, but what I had not prepared myself for was the reaction of the crowd in Mallory Square. Just as the sun set, cameras whirred, small lights flashed and hundreds of voices cheered the vivid colours on the horizon. It certainly was spectacular; I would even go as far to say it was fantastic, but many in the crowd felt there were no superlatives strong enough to express its greatness. Being a newspaper man, I was a little suspicious and even began to wonder whether the publicity men had conned a contract with the celestial authorities.

My programme was quite definite: a sunset every evening was guaranteed; what's more, it was free. The artists and those who admire natural beauty are well catered for. So also is the adventurer, the explorer, the aquatic fanatic, the shell gatherer and fisherman, not forgetting the sun worshipper. The last mentioned is particularly fortunate. Having passed through Venice, where the canals seem to outnumber the streets, we stopped for the evening in Naples. Here I was informed by an exuberant local that Miami beach on the opposite coast was small fry indeed and could be very expensive, while in his part of the world there were forty miles of the best sand anywhere, sun bathing was free and any sharks around swam in their own environment.

Regarding sharks, I will leave this to my fisherman friends to explore for themselves. All I can say is that from shrimp to shark that part of the Gulf of Mexico has a reputation for excellence. For the explorer and adventurer, the Everglades and the Big Cyprus Swamp are well worth a visit. Having spent a day at Marco Island, Neal booked a helicopter flight for the following morning to Key West. After breakfasting at our hotel, the Marriot's Resort, we were airborne within the hour. As we flew southwards the pilot told me that we were passing over the Big Cyprus Swamp and, being a very friendly type, he said that if I had in mind an exploration of the swamp, I would be well advised to use the services of a Seminole Indian guide. He added cheerily: 'Just last week, Mister, a snowbird was badly mauled by a bear.' To me it seemed ridiculous that a ptarmigan or snow grouse could be caught unawares by a relatively clumsy bear and I saw no reason why I should be perturbed. Neal's smile and laconic reply was not reassuring. 'A snowbird, Wil, is the name we give to a pale-faced incomer or tourist from the Northern States. We can only hope the poor man has recovered.' He was diplomatic enough to say nothing about panthers and other dangerous animals that frequented the swamp.

Passing over the Everglades, I gained the impression that the land below was a mixture of Russian steppe and American prairie, or, as some guide books call it, 'a sea of grass'. This, I think, is apt enough, for it is essentially an enormous waterway and the 'grass' was in the main areas of mangrove and similar vegetation. To seawards I could see great hummocks of the same material and was informed that these were called clumps and designated the 'ten thousand islands'.

As we flew into Key West my thoughts were still with the Everglades, and knowing that I might never be so close again, I felt I should at least pay them a short visit. I am certainly not an explorer and I viewed with some apprehension the prospect of having to defend myself against a panther or bear, but as the statistics indicate that the tourist was more likely to encounter a raccoon, I felt extremely brave and curious. It was just after witnessing the remarkable sunset at Key West that I told Neal of my desire. He was enthusiastic and told me he had already arranged a special tour of the Everglades.

He had decided that the best way to link up with the tour was to drive by car to Key Largo. Normally the journey would take three or four hours, but it was his intention to make the journey leisurely, taking as many days, so as to ensure that his passenger would enjoy the experience of having travelled over the most unique road in America. I cannot readily remember the names of the keys or islands we passed on our way to Key Largo, but it certainly was a unique and wonderful experience. Each key, and there were twenty-six of them from Key West to Key Largo, had its own historical background and speciality.

As we passed along this extraordinary part of the M1 highway, Neal gave a running commentary, and in the evenings we dined alfresco where convenient at whichever eating place was recognised by the locals as supplying the best traditional food available. That Neal had travelled this road before was significant. Almost everyone he approached greeted him in a friendly fashion, and it seemed inevitable that as we finished the meal a local worthy would appear, glass in hand, and with due deference enquire if he could join us. As we drank together, our new-found friend would give us his version of what things were like in the past, what they were now, and what could be expected in the near future. It was essentially a medley or pot-pourri of history, economics, literature and local doggerel. Smugglers, pirates, soldiers of fortune, entrepreneurs and engineers played a prominent part in the life of the Keys. Even film stars stole their way into the picture, with well-known writers like Zane Grey and Hemingway being woven into the fabric of the Keys society whether they wanted it or not.

For the next three evenings the theme was the same, but when we reached Key Largo there was a slight but significant variation. The local worthy on this occasion was an old man in his eighties, who insisted that as far as he was concerned he was still a Rock Harbor man. It appeared that the town had been named after John Huston, a film maker, who had shot some scenes of the famous Bogart/Bacall survival saga on the 'African Queen'. The popularity of Bogart had spurred some influential individuals to acquire the river boat 'African Queen' and display it where everyone could see it. The old man, a fan of Humphrey Bogart, was incensed and gave vent to his feelings: 'Those sons of bitches brought the African Queen to the town for their own purposes; now that they are finished with it, the folk of Rock Harbor are left with a rotting eyesore.'

From Key Largo or Rock Harbor we set sail for Flamingo and the Everglades. Neal was in high spirits, evidently looking forward to our trip through the Everglades. Looking at me pensively he asked, 'I hope you enjoyed our wee jaunt down the West Coast Wil?' I laughed at the idea of a wee jaunt and hastened to add that the holiday had been an outstanding success. The scenery of the West Coast had been breathtaking, the people we had met had been friendly and very interesting. As he smilingly nodded approval, I added that this also applied to our flight from

Marco Island to Key West and the remarkable journey up through the Keys to Key Largo, particularly the crossing of the Seven Mile Bridge.

It was at this point that I felt that Neal was worthy of a special mention. 'It has been a wonderful experience to sit comfortably in a car driven by a careful and considerate driver and absorb to the full the feeling as I travelled on a roadway sixty-five feet above the waves of the Atlantic Ocean on one side and the Mexican Gulf on the other.' As Neal's belly laugh subsided, he excused his undue levity and thought fit to explain.

'You must excuse me, Wil, it was the look of innocent wonder on your face as you described the Seven Mile Bridge in romantic terms that set me off. I certainly do appreciate your kind remarks and know you have done your homework.' When I showed him a rather bulky and comprehensive guidebook on Florida loaned me by Neal junior, he laughed again and added, 'It appears my son was looking a little further ahead; I wondered where that book had gone.'

The Everglades tour was an outstanding success and I soon discovered Neal had done his homework. Starting from Flamingo we travelled northwards to Marco Island by easy stages, using appropriate tours in the process. As the natives in the area invariably refer to their habitat as the Wet Lands, I had anticipated being decked out in waterproofs, but hoped it would not be necessary to don a diving suit. It was with relief and pleasure that Neal and I and forty others boarded a tramcar for a two-hour tour through a mangrove forest. The bird watchers among us were enthralled and I felt reasonably happy that the driver, an exceptionally intelligent fellow, had brought mosquito repellant with him. As could be expected, most of our excursions were by boat, ranging from river boat to airboat and canoe. The river boat type of travel suited my mood, allowing me to relax and marvel at the expertise of the Captain, invariably a Seminole Indian, who would navigate through enveloping mangrove with consummate ease. The highlight to me was the sudden emergence from these narrow channels to open water and seeing more clearly the wild life of the area.

I'm no ornithologist, but I did admire and was amused by the wading birds, finding the egrets most attractive. The alligators were a most snooty lot, their noses rising above the surface as they glided along. Somehow I felt they could be dangerous, but the Captain shook his head and, producing a two-and-a-half-foot baby alligator from a tank, put it in my hands. I found it slightly damp but a pleasurable experience to support it gently in my hands. As it looked at me lovingly, I wondered if its mother would have approved.

Cruising through the estuaries we saw bigger animal life. Apart from those smooth merchants, the alligators, nosing around, dolphins would pop up from time to time to entertain and the somnolent manatee or 'seacow' would barely break the surface and just as shyly disappear. The Seminole in charge would from time to time manoeuvre the boat close to a fringe of the mangrove forest and there to greet us would be a clan of those bushy-tailed raccoons, nervously but expectantly holding out their paws, their pointed noses twitching as they wondered what type of largesse these peculiar humans were donating this time round. It was on this occasion that Neal suggested we should try to vary things a little and do something on our own. We decided to hire a canoe for the day and set out to explore the small islands in the vicinity. The idea was a good one, allowing us to appreciate and enjoy the beauty of the tropical plant life and bird life close at hand, something that could only be done from a canoe or similar craft. As we neared the estuary a small problem arose. We had paddled a considerable distance up an inviting channel when suddenly, in a most narrow-minded fashion, it had decided to become impenetrable. Neal was – annoyingly – quite light hearted. 'Well,

Wil,' he said 'I guess I've led you up the creek this time. I'm afraid we'll get more than our feet wet.' It was, of course, only a detail, but it kept us laughing for the rest of the day. Suddenly I was young again, but instead of imagining I was exploring tropical islands, here I was doing it for real – well almost. There were many clumps of mangrove forest, though some had only one solitary tree. In size they varied from a small village to a roadway roundabout, but there was no screeching of petrol-fed monsters, only egrets circling peacefully above, doing their own thing. At the end of the day I was well satisfied and Neal, an Olympic canoeist, awarded me eight points out of ten for paddling.

As we neared Everglades City, Neal opted for a full-day tour, ensuring that when it terminated we would not be too far from Marco Island. We were guided through the Big Cyprus Swamp and, remembering what the helicopter pilot said on our way to Key West, I kept my eyes wide open but have still to encounter a Florida bear or panther. Our guide, a Seminole Indian, assured me they do exist, but possibly they were shy that day. I did discover, however, that Indians lived in great numbers in the Swamp, as they did in the rest of the Everglades. They had lived there for countless centuries, despite the incursions of Spanish and English adventurers.

After being 'swamped', it seemed an anticlimax to board a propane gas-powered tramcar, which transported us deeply into the interior. On the way it stopped at an observation tower, some fifty feet high, where we could view what was known as the sea of grass. This consisted of tall tropical reeds nurtured by the swamp and stretching as far as the eye could see. I was surprised when the guide told me that a thirty-minute boat trip could be exciting. As we stepped into the boat, I envisaged us being well and truly stuck in the mud. Within seconds we were airborne; at least we were skimming over the grass at an exceptional speed. Had the guide mentioned the word airboat, I would have understood, for the boat, in my estimation, was in effect a small seaplane, not designed to fly off into space, but certainly making it feel like it. Although disturbing for the first few seconds, I must concede it was a most exhilarating and enjoyable experience. After lunching at an Indian village, we made tracks in the direction of Marco Island and spent another evening in Marriot's Resort.

In the morning, as we returned to Neal's place, I thought of the highlights of a most interesting and exciting holiday and notched in my memory those experiences I wished to remember. I am an amateur when it comes to superlatives, and in any case I am reluctant to be known as an agent for any particular tourist board, but I can assure anyone in any category that a holiday on the West Coast of Florida through the Everglades and finally down the road to Key West can well be the holiday of a lifetime. The guide book loaned to me by Neal junior was a mine of information, collated in such a way that even I could understand it. To me the holiday was a wonderful experience and I feel the least I can do for anyone interested is to leave the name and address of this most excellent guide book with my publisher. When we entered the Munro abode, Neal junior greeted us enthusiastically and after settling down with drinks, he focused attention on me. There was just the vestige of a smirk as he outlined the procedure he had adopted when seeking information on my behalf concerning the activities of Lucius Chancitt, an American citizen of ill repute. There could be little doubt that Neal junior was a smart cookie, who, by using modern techniques and good contacts, had succeeded in advancing the investigations.

Three days later I left Florida and flew to Italy. I had previously established that after reaching Montevideo, Chancitt had managed to book a passage to Italy, no doubt still hoping to contact Pierre le Blanc. Although I knew the address of the noble family of Chancitts in England, courtesy of Hector Macdonald the lawyer in Kerryville, I still wanted to trace his path to perdition. In Italy I discovered that he had failed to contact his former compatriot and his attempt to infiltrate and establish himself among the middlemen of the drug trade had failed miserably.

Remembering the words of Collette at Cedar Keys in Florida, I realised that for good or ill Chancitt had at last caught up with Pierre le Blanc in France. On the assumption that he had strangled the young woman, I thought it wise to steer clear of the police and concentrate my investigations among the criminal élite. Knowing my investigations would be time consuming, I thought fit to cover my expenses by faxing my editor, indicating that as the monetary union negotiations were reaching a critical stage, I felt I should offer my services should he think fit. Being a good editor and an even better friend, he replied: 'You are on the payroll, Wil, payment by results as usual.'

For three weeks, as the accredited political journalist of the *Morning Sun*, I moved among the eurocrats and managed to satisfy my editor with newsworthy material. With politicians being the natural prey for the criminally minded, it was not long before the feedback gave me the opportunity I required. I had made it known to anyone who would listen that I was interested in the history and development of pharmaceuticals, particularly products used in anaesthesia over the centuries. In the main, I must admit, I was given a coy look or told to get lost by some uncouth people. However, there was one eurocrat who represented a part of his country where the chemical industry was paramount and employed thousands of workers. Wishing to ensure that he was kept in the picture, he decided I might serve his interests, and he introduced me to an old retired pharmacist. He was a bluff old character whose loquaciousness increased relative to his absinthe intake. He seemed inordinately fond of his father, despite referring to him as an old rogue. Before the night was out, I discovered that his father, a distinguished chemist, had unfortunately become enmeshed in the affairs of what can best be described as the non-ethical pharmaceutical industry. Realising rather late that his skills were being prostituted and the gain thereof offset many times over by the pain and misery it inflicted on human society, he decided to end his connection with the illicit drug traffickers. It had not been easy. His life was threatened many times and in the end he had changed sides and had been responsible for the imprisonment of leading drug traffickers. His father, he said, had been quite sanguine over the whole affair and told him, 'If I don't expose them, they will kill me.' His father had mentioned the name of Pierre le Blanc as a handsome French Canadian who had arrived on the scene rather late. I took the opportunity to ask the man if his father had known of a man named Chancitt. The old pharmacist paled visibly, turned in his seat to ensure that no-one was within hearing distance, and putting a finger to his lips, issued a warning: 'Don't mention his name around here, M'sieur, it could be dangerous.'

After assuring him that I knew Chancitt to be a criminal who could not be trusted even by his own kind, the old pharmacist relaxed and quietly continued. Although the criminal élite had respect for Pierre, they had left him in no doubt that the 'black scarecrow' was definitely persona non grata. The day after the young girl was found strangled, Chancitt had disappeared. If the drug smugglers had caught him, they would certainly have killed him. The following day Pierre, having been associated too closely with Chancitt, found it necessary to transfer his operations across the Channel. It appeared his exit had been opportune, for a smuggler, the original leader of the gang and also owner of a brothel, had discovered that his top-earning prostitute had been cruelly suffocated and defiled. All the evidence appeared to point in the direction of the American. Although I already knew

Chancitt was a womaniser and a treacherous criminal, I now knew I was on the belated trail of a monster. I was now completely satisfied that Chancitt had no option but to make for the home of his ancestors.

CHAPTER 6

It was in the fell country twixt Cumbria and Durham in the North of England that I discovered the mouldering ruins of what had at one time been the stronghold of the Chancitts. Having registered for breakfast at the Fell Inn, I decided a stroll in the gloaming towards the old house might be rewarding. I suppose it was the romantic in me, hoping in the twilight to imagine, or even see, something reminiscent of the good old days of chivalry. I should have known better. Instead all I saw among the ruins was rubbish: a mass of discarded bottles, empty cans and, in the most unlikely places, deflated condoms. The only piece of wood left was a decaying oak transom, on which a message had been sprayed with an aerosol. The level of intelligence of the last transient tribe was significant: 'Coca Cola rules here, OK.' As I pondered the depravity of some of today's youth, I heard a movement just behind me. In the failing light I could just make out two ruddy cheeks floating towards me, much of the body and legs obscured by a swirling ground mist. The deerstalker hat had signalled a man of the open spaces. As he drew abreast, I could see the twinkling eyes of a hale and hearty son of the soil.

Before I could speak he introduced himself. 'I'm Tom Smart, a farmer in this area and just in case you are interested, Mister, the ruins in front of you are what is left of Chancitt House.' Introducing myself, I thanked him and made him aware that I was interested in the history of the Chancitts, but I deplored the vandalism that had taken place. Before he could wax too eloquent

71

on the tortures that should be inflicted on vandals, I intervened and suggested that I would be grateful if he would accompany me back to the Fell Inn for a beverage or two, where, if so inclined, he could tell me more concerning the history of the Chancitts.

He beamed a smile, shook my hand and demonstrating his acute sense of humour, said, 'I'm willing, and of course you are Wil Ling.' I spent a pleasant evening listening to a man well versed in English history and, being also an accomplished raconteur, he was able to make a dull topic sparkle a little without demeaning his subject. Later I was to learn that Tom Smart lived up to his name when the landlord informed me that Tom was the best after-dinner speaker in the county. Tom's knowledge of the Chancitts had come *via* his father and grandfather. It appeared the family had lorded it from the time of William the Conqueror, but from the start of the twentieth century their power had rapidly diminished. It had been the classic example of a rich and powerful family losing its place in the rat race. The lazy, the inept and those who had blotted the family escutcheon had been sent packing to the colonies, to survive on an ever-diminishing remittance. Those too clever by half had disappeared before the police could apprehend them.

The only remaining member of the family, the Dowager Duchess Marie Louise, who was made of sterner stuff, had struggled on. Determined to re-establish the family name to near its former glory, and hopefully to a state of financial stability, she engaged the services of an extremely clever young lawyer named Nicholas Quarefellow, who managed to manoeuvre the stately home of the Chancitts, the estate and the adjoining land into the National Trust, thus clearing up estate duty and other little items due to the nation. For this he ultimately received a knighthood. Having salvaged the family name, Louise felt comforted but the state of near penury was distressing. Having heard of her plight, the ladies of the local Conservative Gentlewomen's Society rushed to her aid. After all, for many years she had been a generous contributor to their funds. Having heard of the sordid financial details, they deigned to take tea with her, demolished what was left of the larder, complimented her on her home baking, and then in the most genteel manner advised her that under the circumstances the best she could do would be to get lost. The Salvation Army was more humane and practical. They attended to her immediate needs and set in train enquiries regarding the whereabouts of relatives and friends who could help the Duchess. No member of the Chancitt family could be traced and it appeared they had vanished from the earth. How Louise and her personal maid established a profitable teashop is another story.

But that was not the end of the Chancitt story. Tom Smart's grandfather had told him that two years later an American had walked into the Fell Inn and introduced himself as the son of Lord Chancitt. On being told what had become of the family fortune and realising the vultures had destroyed his inheritance, he had controlled his chagrin, and although tempted to throw away his documents, he had kept them to prove he was an American offshoot of the family who had arrived just too late to clear the family name. He had boasted that had he arrived in time, he was sure he could, with his American know-how, have made Chancitt Manor a going concern.

A year later a rather excited farmer had come back from Newcastle with news of Chancitt. After finishing his business, he had gone down to the waterfront and had been surprised to see a sign above a shop: 'Chancitt Shipchandler'. Visiting the local pub, owned by his nephew, he had heard some startling rumours. It appeared that Chancitt had done quite well from shipping orders but probably more from smuggling. Although this was accepted as something normal, it was to be deplored that his main money-spinner was drugs.

Next morning I, like Lucius Chancitt, left the Fell Inn for

Newcastle, only I was eighty years behind him. My investigations showed that after some months of relatively honest trading, he had heard of something that could be to his advantage. It could, if true, turn out risky but profitable. He had tolerated ship chandling during the daytime so long as it did not interfere with his night school activities in the nether regions of the pubs in Newcastle's dockland.

One evening, while in the company of a rather talkative American sailor, he had learned that the man had 'gotten his fix' from someone called Peter. Further prodding revealed that Peter was a runner operating on behalf of the local cocaine dispenser, who, it appeared, had boasted that the real boss was a man called Snow White. Chancitt realised that if the story was true, this could be his opportunity to get back into the big time.

The name Snow White conjured up the image of the rather large French Canadian who had been his partner in crime. He knew from experience he had to be patient. He could not rely on an American drunk, but felt that the matter should be pursued. He made a point of contacting the sailor several times before the ship left Newcastle. Supplying him with the beverage which made him most loquacious, he questioned and listened most attentively. He learned the names, the descriptions and habits of the people with whom the sailor had associated prior to getting his 'fix'.

Lucius continued his night school studies and after two days and nights of alcoholic injections into the mouths of some of the more disreputable characters in the bar, he found himself talking with a rather insignificant reject of the human race. What he had to say was of great significance to Lucius and led to a meeting the following evening with the man called Peter. Peter was a rather overdressed fidgety man, who it appeared was a runner for the local bookmaker.

After four large whiskies, he admitted he was more concerned with the coca stakes than the winner at Epsom or Ascot. Lucius smiled horribly at the flashily dressed runner; it was something which came quite natural. Putting his arm round the man's shoulders, he drew him close in the most companionable way and spoke low and slow. 'I appreciate your humour, son, but being in the trade myself, the only fix that I'm interested in is fixing a meeting with your immediate boss or Snow White himself.' The man visibly wilted and stammered something which was incoherent. Knowing he had reached a crucial stage, Lucius felt he had to placate him. Advising him to relax, he assured him he had everything to gain. All he had to do was to mention the name Chancitt and he would be on a real winner.

It was a nervous man who left Lucius that night, but the reaction which quickly followed could only be described as dramatic. The following night a well-built serious looking man walked straight over to Lucius and, looking at him inquiringly, dropped a card on the table. 'Mr Chancitt?' he said in a firm voice. Taken aback, Lucius could only nod. He heard the words, 'Your invitation, sir,' and the man was gone, disappearing as quickly as he had come. The card was an invitation to visit the Snow White restaurant in Carlisle. The card laid claim to being the top restaurant in the North of England, serving the best main meal anywhere, followed by a sweet one would never forget.

Chancitt felt like running after the messenger and demanding an explanation, but he controlled his anxiety, knowing that this was the type of unorthodox touch that could be expected from Snowy. It could be a hoax, but he felt he had no option but to make the journey to Carlisle. A cold easterly was blowing as he trudged through the snow-clogged streets of the town. He was cold and miserable and beginning to doubt if he was on the right track when he saw through the swirling snow a sign in coloured lights. When he drew near, he knew he had reached his destination. Half a minute later the black-clothed cadaverous figure of Lucius Chancitt burst into the bright and welcoming atmosphere of Snowy's place.

It was a revelation even to Lucius, who had in the past conducted business in some class joints. But this was for real; after all, many of the furnishings on the American continent had been imported from Britain and Europe. It was the set-up that impressed him; he had not expected such luxury in a small town. The warmth also was most acceptable, considering the cold and misery he had suffered since leaving Newcastle.

At this stage I felt instinctively that the Chancitt investigation was nearing a climax, knowing that the mind of the cocaine dispenser and womaniser was such that he would not survive the pleasures of the brothel and cocaine to which he himself had become addicted. It is normal for an investigator to seek information from the local and national authorities, particularly if the subject concerned had resided in the area some eight years before. On the other hand the local library or news office could well be worth a visit. As could be expected, the Snow White Restaurant and pleasure centre had disappeared long before.

Having the intelligence to make haste for the local tavern, I was fortunate in meeting an old compositor, who knew that ale was invented centuries before by the monks and other religious orders. Also, and more to the purpose, he knew most of the headlines of his paper over the last century. By the end of the evening it was agreed that he would arrange a visit to the small records museum of his paper. It took twenty minutes to unearth the paper I was looking for.

On the twenty-fifth of February 1913 the headline was dramatic: 'SNOW WHITE'S SEX ORGY'. It appeared that the gossip columnist had managed to secrete himself in the inner confines of the pleasure centre as a piece of furniture or a potential customer. Whichever camouflage or ploy he used, he had been able to witness some remarkable happenings before the police raided the place.

The information given by the columnist was quite elaborate. I felt sure the central character could only be Lucius Chancitt and this is what took place. On entering the pleasure centre, a beautiful blonde girl had approached him, and in a voice that was soft and pleasant had asked him if she could be of assistance. He produced the invitation, whereupon she gave him a radiant smile and asked him to accompany her. Once seated, she informed him that Snowy was looking forward to seeing him. Unfortunately, however, there would be a delay. Would he therefore be kind enough to accept the hospitality of the house for a short time until things were adjusted?

He relaxed and enjoyed the excellent fare of the establishment. The atmosphere of bonhomie was extremely relaxing, even soporific. He awakened to a voice announcing the presence of Snow White. Looking up as if in a dream, he saw the figure of a woman in full bloom dressed in white satin, the material clinging to a generous body, her breasts trying to be discreet as they peeped through the lace work of a rather low cut creation. Mischievous eyes fixed directly on him, red lips opened and a husky contralto voice flowed forth. 'You seem disappointed, Monsieur.'

It was a dilemma. Expecting to see Pierre, he now found himself confronted by a woman who, as far as he was concerned, was most desirable. Although befuddled and puzzled, he felt it only sensible to avail himself of all that the house had to offer. He answered the voluptuous creature in front of him accordingly. 'Madame, I must apologise if you feel I am disappointed – far from it. I am delighted though possibly disorientated. I had not expected to see someone so alluring and so attentive and attuned to what a man might desire.'

Madame smiled, gave a little gurgle of delight, and asked him if he wished to sample the special sweet course. Nodding expectantly, he followed her one floor up, where she hoped his wish might be granted. He found himself in an octagonal shaped hall, in the centre of which, forming a hub, were eight sumptuously furnished sofas on which customers could relax while making up their minds which sweet they desired. Radiating from the centre were eight carpeted pathways of different colours, at the end of which were eight doors.

Each door displayed a full scale picture of the desirable maiden within. Madame linked her arm in his and gave a conducted tour, explaining that each lady served up a confection appropriate to the caption on the door. Number one was hot chocolate, reflected by her vibrant brown body and dark burning eyes. There were seven more, sufficient choice to satisfy the most fastidious. Strawberry Blonde, Black Magic, and for those innocent enough to think they had the stamina, there was always Green Ginger Greta from the Northern Hemisphere. For those more mature men who knew their limitations and wished to relax, Lulu Bye Bye from Polynesia could be relied on to nurse them through their hour of delight. As the tour ended, she nudged him in the ribs gently, in a ladylike manner, telling him that as a special guest he could, without charge, press the bell that suited him.

Lucius was given no time to reply; with a swish of skirts she was gone. He was in a quandary. His mission was to meet Pierre. On the other hand he was enjoying himself, and saw no reason why he should not accept all that was being offered; there was no time like the present. Pictured on one door was a Latin beauty captioned 'French Frolic'. He pondered for a few seconds, then rang the bell. Almost immediately the door opened, and a saucy character straight from the Folies Bergères beckoned him in. Taking him by the hand, she led him over to an ornate upholstered plinth all set for action.

The red luscious lips moved. 'I am ready, monsieur, unless it is a man you want.' Taken aback, he snapped, 'What d'ya mean? I'm no queer. Just you lay back, girlie.' As she stretched out, she looked invitingly at him, but there was something about her that puzzled him. The impasse lasted a few seconds while his brain and loins sorted out priorities. As he moved towards the plinth a stentorian voice in low key broke the silence. 'Welcome to the play centre, Lucius.'

Standing in front of him was Pierre le Blanc, resplendent in evening dress. Although taken aback and disconcerted by Pierre's dramatic appearance, he reacted quickly. He looked at his erstwhile companion in crime and admitted: 'You look a million dollars, Pierre, but why the play acting?' Turning to the girl on the plinth, he apologised. 'Sorry, baby, you sure are gorgeous, a'm thinkin' we could have done things together, but business is business.' Regarding it as a personal slight, the young prostitute gave him a withering look and replied in a voice full of scorn: 'Get lost.'

Lucius, who seemed oblivious to the scathing riposte, looked inquiringly at Pierre and asked, 'Well, Snowy, am I welcome in this wonderland of yours or must I wander further?' Snowy smiled charmingly and replied, 'Let us retire to my private den and discuss the past, the present, and, who knows, even the future.'

It was soon clear to Lucius Chancitt that Snowy had no intention of assisting him unless he could show that he had some realistic collateral. As the conversation became desultory, Lucius lost patience with the grinning French Canadian and gave vent to his inner feelings. 'Stop buggering about, Snowy, are you going to help a friend or not?' Their friendship, based mainly on business, was obviously tenuous and becoming more fragile by the minute. Snowy reacted accordingly. 'O.K., Lucius, let's finish with the small talk. If you want a piece of the action, how much are you prepared to invest?' Lucius knew there would be no handout; he had to control himself and be content with some sort of deal.

It was surely one of life's ironies that just as the two crooks reached an agreement, the sharp blast of police whistles sounded and all hell seemed to break loose. There was a crashing of doors and furniture, the screams and curses of prostitutes being denied their vocation, and the sorrowful spectacle of some of the nation's dignitaries whining and yelping as they were caught with their pants down. It was little solace to know that one of the Royals, with a penchant for that type of relaxation, had also been caught.

By the time the police forced their way into the inner sanctum, Pierre was ready to deal with the situation in a dignified manner. It mattered little; they were both escorted to the local police station together with all who were thought to have been involved in libidinous behaviour. Lucius claimed he had been invited to meet the proprietor, Pierre or Peter White, to discuss the sale of imported wines. As a shipchandler, exporter and importer in Newcastle, it was normal for him not to ignore a business opportunity. When he produced his family documents and passport, the police telephoned Newcastle, who inadvertently gave him a clean bill of health.

After belated enquiries, the Newcastle police discovered that shipchandler Chancitt was also a drug trafficker. Unfortunately by this time Lucius had decided to become absent without leave. I knew now Lucius Chancitt was running out of time, out of space and out of corners in which to hide. The old compositor must have seen the look on my face and asked, 'Well, mister, are you satisfied?' Pursing my lips and looking at him tentatively and appealingly, I replied: 'Not quite. Tomorrow perhaps?' He seemed agreeable to the suggestion that we should meet again in the evening at his local.

It was again an enjoyable evening, as both of us were scholars, so that we had no difficulty in solving the world's problems over a pint or two. Next morning we returned to the local depository of information and knowledge. Starting from the 'Snow White

Scandal' of 25 February, I scanned as patiently and methodically as I could the day-by-day and month-by-month events in the area. My companion, having a macabre sense of humour, stuck in the main to the deaths column, making me aware from time to time what he considered to be amusing headstone scripts. When we reached July he suddenly shouted, 'Eureka!'

The name Chancitt was certainly in the death column, but the cause of death was not noted. A charitable trust in the North of England had thought fit to ask any relatives or friends to contact them. Realising the hospice might have closed its doors at some time in the dim past, I made tracks for the local registry office. Having established he had died, I was given directions regarding the site of the hospice and was assured that it was still carrying on the good work despite the gerrymandering of the Conservative government.

The main building was of red sandstone, constructed at the beginning of the twentieth century, and bore the hallmark of expert craftsmanship. To me it still looked new and I hoped that some idiot in the Health Ministry would not close the door before I reached it. When I asked to see the manager, the receptionist gave me a queer look and I, realising that the privateers had not yet wormed their way in, reassured her that I was only interested in something that had happened long ago. She brightened up and told me Doctor Galbraith and Matron McIver were extremely busy, but possibly Mrs McAllister, the Lady Almoner, could help me.

Mary McAllister, a bonny Scot, seemed agreeable and ready to help. But when I told her I only wanted some information, she reacted acutely and scowled as she asked, 'You're not from the Ministry of Health, I hope?' I allayed her suspicions immediately, assuring her that as an investigative journalist I was concerned with the behaviour pattern of a drug smuggler and wished to know how Lucius Chancitt had died in July 1913. She smiled sweetly, apologised, and saw fit to explain that the hospice had been bedeviled by government officials and so-called medical trusts who were obviously more concerned with profits than people. As I nodded my approval, she continued: 'I have heard of you, Mr Ling, and applaud what you have done in exposing the seamier side of this government's behaviour, and I am sure that any information you obtain is for a worthy cause.'

Twenty minutes later she returned with the information I wanted. She had been thorough in her search. 'It would appear, Mr Ling,' she said, 'that Mr Ignatius Lucius Chancitt, an American, was brought to the hospice by ambulance on 2 July 1913. He was in very poor shape, suffering from advanced syphilis and cocaine addiction. His condition deteriorated rapidly and he died from venereal infection and cocaine poisoning some three weeks later.'

I thought it only fair to seek her approval, and asked, 'Would you agree with me, Miss McAllister, that a mention in my column of the miserable death of a drug smuggler from a lethal cocktail of syphilis and cocaine might alert the public to the extreme danger of participating in indiscriminate sex and the taking of drugs?' She nodded agreement and wished me well. As I thanked her for the support she had given, she thought fit to encourage me further. 'Quite some time ago, Mr Ling, you wrote about a government minister who deprived many thousands of children of their school milk, and from that, about a government ultimately pledged to a policy of deregulation. This, as could be expected, led to the deprivation of millions of adults. Unemployment was rife, the crooks of society prospered, the rich grew richer at the expense of the poor. Shady deals became normal as pension funds were robbed, and the government, in its attempt to quell the anger of the people, invoked their god of private enterprise to be merciful.'

Although respecting her opinion, I intervened, knowing that I could be a prisoner for the rest of the day. As she reached the phrase 'God of private enterprise', I complimented her. 'Miss McAllister, you are obviously a meticulous reader of politics; I noticed you stressed the word "their" as opposed to "the"!' Her smile was mischievous as she replied: 'Mr Ling, the common people, and I am one of them, know full well that the god of the present government is one of appeasing and furthering private enterprise, and only God or the good of the people can supplant it.' Her militancy and intelligence shook me and before I could reply she added that the column headed 'From Rickets to Rackets' was most appropriate; certainly the common people knew that the lady concerned had shown little sign of the milk of human kindness. When I left Miss McAllister, I assured her I would do my best to make the young aware of the misery and danger of drug addiction.

As I travelled by train to the Metropolis and my cubby-hole in the offices of the *Morning Sun*, I took stock of the last half year. Why had I spent so much time investigating the life of a small time crook, when I could have been absorbed in playing a part in exposing the unhealthy and dangerous manipulations of the death merchants as they made deals with their subterranean allies in the various Ministries of Defence? I had little doubt that in the near future I would use the material gathered for a constructive purpose, but I felt somehow that my investigations had in the main been more subjective than objective, probably because I was involved to some degree in a personal way.

I was agreeably surprised when my editor congratulated me on the material I had supplied while on holiday in the Americas and Europe. He felt, however, that I should have been on the spot during the 'Arms to Iran' scandal, but was prepared to forgive if I boarded a plane for the Middle East and sent back some real news concerning any pitfalls that might arise during the peace conference between the Arabs and Jews. Being Wil Ling,

I did my best and was fortunate to be able to report that the peacemakers on both sides were nosing ahead of the merchants of death.

CHAPTER 7

Mission accomplished, I was called back to cover a conference of the European Nations to be held in Edinburgh. Reaching the Scottish capital a few days before the great event, I decided to contact the author of the novel, Sorenson. It was an interesting and enjoyable meeting. The old author had taken the trouble to trace my movements through the political snippets and dispatches I sent from time to time to my paper from the various trouble spots where I had found myself. He had even learned of my presence in Kerryville, USA, from his pen friend Hector McDonald. 'So you see, Mr Ling,' he said, 'although I appreciate your search for the truth, I am still mystified as to why you should have taken so much trouble to investigate the wrong-doings of a rogue while on holiday in the Americas. I can only trust your pilgrimage was successful.'

I conceded he had a point, but assured him I had no religious tendencies. I was certainly not a pilgrim. It was something personal that motivated me, something which had still to be clarified. I reminded him that he had originally told me that his father had mentioned the name Chancitt or Lord Chancitt, but never the full name, Ignatius Lucius Chancitt, the name which he had used in the novel. He smiled as he admitted that the first draft contained only the word Chancitt, but at a conference of writers he had met Hector and asked him if he had ever heard of the name. Some time later Hector had sent him a letter informing him that his lawyer father had in his files the name of Lord

Chancitt and a son Ignatius Lucius, born 25 July, 1885. He laughed as he chided me. 'Hector might never have known that I used the full name in a work of fiction had it not been for your investigative prowess. However, he has forgiven me and asked that should you contact me again, I was to give you his kind regards.' I responded accordingly and asked him to tell Hector that I had enjoyed his company.

As the old man nodded, I asked if he was prepared to tolerate another question or two. He was very bright, obviously enjoying himself and blithely replied, 'Fire ahead, lad, we all need to learn.' During our first meeting he had told me that the main character, a seaman called Sorenson, was based on his father. Although fictional, much of the material had been drawn from similar incidents associated with his father. I took issue with the name Pierre le Blanc, alias Peter White or Snowy, telling him that although the character was cast as fictional, it was, as the Americans would say, for real. He smiled indulgently towards me and asked to be allowed to set the record straight. 'Let's fill our glass, Mr Ling, then sit back and I will tell you a story.'

I sat back as instructed, knowing that whatever the content, the old author could be relied on to make it interesting. Having laid the foundation for his novel, he decided to relax in the beautiful English Lake District. At the hotel in which he stayed he found himself in the company of anglers and other tellers of tall yarns. It was most opportune that the man who befriended him was a retired Inspector of Police, who had read and appreciated his work. The Inspector admitted to being 'a chip off the old block', his father having been Chief of Police in Carlisle. He had asked the Inspector if he had ever heard the name Chancitt being mentioned. The Inspector had shaken his head, but later in the evening remembered that many years ago he had read that Lady Chancitt, the last member of an old aristocratic family, had been forced, through lack of funds, to leave the ancestral home.

Just as they were about to retire, the Inspector ordered another round, explaining that he had thought of something rather special. As a teenager, his father had ensured that he was properly equipped to face the world. He had warned him against taking drugs, drinking in bad company and the danger of indulging in illicit sex. As if to warn him, he had told him about a police raid on a brothel which had shocked the nation. A French Canadian named Pierre le Blanc, alias Peter White, had used his restaurant for a well-equipped brothel. During the raid the police had arrested Pierre le Blanc and another man. At this point the Inspector had stopped dramatically and told him that he had remembered the name of the other man.

I felt it was only fair to intervene and tell the author about my investigations in the North of England. He smiled benignly towards me, indicating that since Chancitt had been apprehended in the company of Pierre le Blanc, who had been accused of smuggling drugs, it was only natural that he associated both as partners in cocaine smuggling and trafficking. It mattered little whether they had acted individually or together, but it gave him the opportunity to cast them as villains acting in concert against the best interests of his hero, Sorenson. As I pondered his statement, he continued: 'Now that you have proved that two of the characters in my work of fiction were in fact real, I can only hope that the houses of Chancitt and le Blanc do not sue.'

He was in an expansive mood and anxious to know why a journalist of some standing should take the trouble to investigate the life of a man like Lucius Chancitt. I had to admit that in the first instance it had been his presentation of Chancitt as a most repulsive man that had had me wondering if a man such as this had really walked the earth. He shook his head, reminding me that we were both men of the world. 'Come off it, Mr Ling. Whatever motivated you was something far deeper than a writer's description of an unsavoury American dope pedlar.' As

I hesitated, he followed up: 'Don't tell me that it was because he was implicated in the murdering of women. After all, you only became aware of this during your investigations.'

I held up my hand asking that a truce be observed. Responding readily, he filled my glass, asking as he did so that I should relax, imbibe a little, then tell him my innermost thoughts, should I so desire. I confessed that after our first interview the name Chancitt had haunted me slightly. For almost a week I had mulled over the name, trying to link it with a person or an event I had been involved with in the not too distant past. On the odd occasion the name had rung a bell, but although my hearing seemed normal, my memory was definitely in need of overhaul.

It was about this time that my American cousin rescued me, inviting me to holiday with him at his home in Florida. Accepting readily, I was able to escape the vagaries of London weather and the wails of the people as the government attempted to privatise fresh air. As I relaxed in the sunshine of Florida, my mind switched back to my adventure in South America. Suddenly the name of Chanceet shone through; only time would tell if there was a link. Giving the old author a short resumé of the events that followed, I was able to convince him that Chancitt had fathered Chanceet. Although my search for the truth had taken many months, the old man seemed to appreciate the way I had condensed my findings.

'Mr Ling,' he said, 'your narrative was short and extremely interesting. I'm sure you have in your possession enough material for a first rate novel.' I assured him I was perfectly happy to have solved what to me had been a personal problem; after all Chanceet had saved my life. My vocation had always been one of exposing wrongdoers, and if he thought my investigations were worthy of a novel, I would be only too pleased to hand over my material. As he pursed his lips ready to speak, I took the initiative. 'After all, Mr Sorenson, your father laid the foundation for your novel and influenced you in casting Chancitt as a villain. If you accept my word and proof that Chanceet, the son of a villain, became the hero and protector of his people, I think you might seriously consider using Chanceet as a rather remarkable hero.' As he hesitated, I added, 'After all, Mr Sorenson, you have the original copyright and you could set the record straight.'

My statement surprised the old man, but he responded graciously. Leaning forwards towards me, an arm resting on his desk and beaming, he replied: 'You obviously consider Chanceet to be an exceptionally fine man and should I accept your suggestion, I am sure the result would be an exceptionally fine sequel.' Anxious to know his views on heredity, I asked if he had any knowledge of the functions of genes and chromosomes. He coughed, scratched his chin and conceded he knew more about chronology than chromosomes. Before I could develop my line of thought, he beat me to it. Clearing his throat, he gave an opinion. 'Mr Ling, I know what you are thinking. It matters little what the scientists come up with regarding the prominence of certain genes; for your comfort let us assume that the genes of Chanceet's mother were in the ascendancy.'

I thanked him for his effort in assuring me that the genes of Chanceet's mother had predominated, but I was still interested in how the life of Homo Sapiens could be influenced by external forces. The old author was most obliging and, being in a jocose mood, he tolerated my curiosity. 'I cannot claim to be esoterically inclined, Mr Ling. My knowledge of the occult is indeed limited. I find the claims made for astrology and other mysterious "ologies" to be suspect, apart from numerology which has been perfected by the most successful bookmakers.' I seized the opportunity to intervene. 'Although I would not be inclined to associate you with bookmakers, Mr Sorenson, you did nevertheless say you were acquainted with numerology, which is a product of the occult.' His reply made me feel I was becoming a bit of a bore. 'Come off it, Mr Ling, you know damn well what I mean. The modern bookmaker relies on computer science, not the murmuring of some mystic or priest.' I agreed with him that the subject could be boring and invariably the end result inconclusive, but I still wished to finalise my findings regarding the life of Lucius Chancitt, and as far as I was concerned, dates and numbers seemed to play an uncanny part.

The old author reassured me. 'Carry on, Mr Ling, you seem to have something definite to say; I'm sure it will be interesting.' I started with the date 25 July. He nodded and added, '25 July, 1885, Ignatius Lucius Chancitt was born!' I carried on: 'El Chanceet, son of Chancitt, was born 25 July, 1911.' He raised his eyebrows a little. I then referred to his novel, 'To Emily Sjorgen and Edward Sorenson, a son, born 25 July, 1913.' At this point the old man became excited and beat me to it. He told me that for dramatic presentation he had decided in his novel to eliminate Lucius Chancitt by having him burned in the Leith grain elevator, just as he himself was emerging from his mother's womb. He seemed quite pleased with himself as he gave his opinion. 'That I was born at the time Lucius Chancitt perished has nothing to do with numerology or chronology. As the writer I was responsible for his demise; there was nothing fatalistic about it.' He looked at me for approval. I in turn asked that he should not judge too hastily. Before he could reply, I told him I still had something to say regarding the latter part of my investigations. I knew I had to be careful. If I overstepped the mark, I might easily annoy him and even hurt him emotionally. I referred to my interview with Mrs McAllister at the hospice in the North of England and told him how Chancitt had died from a virulent type of venereal disease and cocaine poisoning. I looked intently at him as I reached the climax: 'The date of death was . . .' He looked startled and before I could finish he almost shouted, 'Don't tell me!' I ignored his interjection and as I nodded I quoted: '25

July, 1913'. I'll be damned,' he said. I tried to reassure him. 'No,' I said, but Lucius Chancitt was.' As he looked quizzically at me, I continued: 'So you see, Mr Sorenson, although you fictionalised his departure from the human race by cremating him in a grain elevator fire at Leith, in reality he died in agony in a North of England hospice.' I allowed him time to compose himself and then asked: 'Well, what do you think?' He looked earnestly at me and replied, 'From a numerology viewpoint I can only assume that his number was up. However, as a writer knowing his background, I would say it was a case of poetic justice. As a defiler of women and an agent of misery and death to his fellow men through cocaine profiteering, he only got what he deserved.'

For the moment there was silence, then he added, 'Poor miserable bugger, instant death by burning would surely have been better than the agony of slow painful disintegration.' Again I allowed time for adjustment before telling him that I had been so impressed by the constant date factor that I had felt it necessary to investigate the time element of what I regarded as mysterious events. In the novel Sorenson revealed that Grangemouth was his birthplace. When I mentioned the place he sat bolt upright, his brow furrowed, and peering through lowered eyebrows, he addressed me in a rather sardonic fashion. 'I know you have been very thorough in your investigations, Mr Ling, but I never considered for a moment that you would deem it worthwhile to look for supernatural manifestations in that small seaport.'

I apologised for being possibly too intrusive, but I was sure that when he heard what I had to say, he would consider my efforts had been worthwhile. There was a flicker of a smile as he again waved his hand, an indication that he, like myself, preferred cerebral activity, adding that as far as he was concerned the only time his number had been called was at a bingo session. As I quoted the date and time of his birth at Basin Street in Grangemouth, he snapped back: 'There was no need for you to travel to Grangemouth; I could have told you that.' Having upset him, I knew I would have to justify my actions. I had taken his novel with me but it was not until I met Hector Macdonald in America that I discovered Lucius Chancitt was 'for real' and no longer fictional. Having notched in my mind his birth date, that of Chancitt and his son Chanceet, the number 25 had become, so to say, a symbol of something most unusual, meriting investigation. He was not amused and certainly not convinced. 'You're wasting our time, Mr Ling,' he said, 'you know what happened to the cat?' I replied that my job, indeed my vocation, was such that curiosity was paramount and I was sure that I still had a few lives left. When I informed him that the actual time of his birth coincided with the death of Lucius Chancitt, he sighed and asked, 'Is all this really necessary?' Confessing that I had also travelled to Leith, his riposte took me completely by surprise. 'Yes, another 25th. My father died in 1929, the day of my sixteenth birthday.' I apologised for having upset him and promised I would not mention that number again, but I felt he would welcome what my investigation had revealed. 'Carry on, Mr Ling,' he replied, 'we can discuss the occult and that mysterious number when we have nothing more useful to do.'

I started where so many tales have their beginning, in a pub in Commercial Street, Leith. According to his novel, his father had met Sven Sjorgen and Rory McLeod and they had adjourned to this particular tavern, just across the road from that massive building, His Majesty's Customs and Excise. Having purchased my beverage in that tavern, I made a point of asking to see the manager. The waiter, a Leither, looked at me strangely and replied: 'I'll tell big Jake you want to see him.' As I sat waiting, my mind conjured up a swarthy Scot in a seaman's jersey, but on looking up, I discovered that Jake, although big, was a well dressed, fair headed Shetlander, who, I soon found out, had settled in Leith and acquired the pub after a lengthy stint as a company porter in the docks. This was good fortune indeed. Coming from the north, his education had not been neglected and his knowledge of local and international affairs proved extensive. He had never seen, but had heard many tales of, Edward Sorenson and associated him with the First World War and the depression that followed. Leaving me abruptly, he turned to a trophy shelf displaying football and bowling cups won by the pub's locals, and picking up a small glass box, brought it to the counter for my inspection. Inside I could see half a pack of playing cards and just above them two quarters of the same pack. As I puzzled over the significance of the display, he pointed to two names engraved on the top of the glass box. They read SORENSON 1 and SAMPSON 2.

As I looked inquiringly at him, he smiled and pointed in the direction of two old men who, he said, would in a year or so be receiving a tribute from her Majesty the Queen. 'Bill and Ben,' he said, 'are not the flowerpot men, but I am sure they will dig up something for you.'

They had just finished playing a hand of dominoes and were discussing who should buy the next round. Apologising for breaking into their negotiations, I told them I was seeking information regarding a Danish seaman they might have known, a man named Sorenson, who operated as a water agent at the time of the First World War. As they cogitated, I hastened to add that big Jake had assured me that if anybody knew, they would.

The two old characters smiled beautifully towards me. Even their teeth, although second generation, seemed to enjoy the experience. Bill, being senior by ten months, welcomed me and, giving a wee cough, indicated they would be only too pleased to accommodate me. Realising his throat was dry, I asked what particular elixir would be appropriate. Duly lubricated, Bill started off, with Ben ready to take over should his companion have a lapse of memory or miss some important detail. Yes, there was a man who fitted my description. About two years before the start of World War One, a Danish seaman had arrived on the scene and quickly established himself as a water agent, operating on the coast from Leith to Grangemouth. Bill thought his name was Sorenson, but they both knew him as Eddie or Edward. He was a popular man in both parts of the pub. As I looked quizzically at Bill, Ben interrupted. 'What Bill means is that in the saloon bar where the sea captains, ship owners and big wigs had their snifters, he was accepted as an equal and they called him Edward. In oor bar the dockers, shipyard workers and seamen spent many a happy time with Eddie.' Bill nodded sagely and continued his story. Eddie was clever and astute, but more importantly he was a good man. His knowledge of languages never ceased to amaze them. During the war when things were difficult to get, Eddie would solve the problem without exploiting anyone. He was recognised by many as a smiling debonair man; if he had any fault it was in being over-generous to those who did not deserve it. When Eddie was around, there was always laughter; if there were arguments to settle or problems to solve, they all looked to Eddie, who seemed to smile his way through them.

It was at this point that I asked about the small glass casket on the display shelf. Ben dug Bill in the ribs and replied: 'We are the only two in the pub to have seen what happened, but I think the honour should be given to the son of one of the contestants to describe that.' Tam, a company porter like his father before him, agreed it was always a story well worth telling. His father Sam had just beaten a Norwegian sailor at hand-wrestling. After he had flattened the Norwegian's arm to the table, the audience had clamoured for another contest. There had been no takers, but Eddie, after undue cajolery, had deferred to the crowd and agreed to challenge the victor. At the beginning he had declined, arguing that it was surely unfair to ask an eleven-stone man to compete against a fifteen-stone expert, but to shouts of 'you can do it Eddie,' he had conceded. There was one condition, however: the contest should take place standing at the bar and not sitting at a table. He walked over and positioned his right elbow on the counter, then, facing Sam, he invited him to do likewise. With their arms in the vertical position they clasped hands and the contest started. Sam immediately moved Eddie's arm a few inches from the vertical, but Eddie, still smiling, seemed content in holding fast. Some three minutes later they were back to square one, but it was noticeable that Eddie was inclined to concentrate on pulling Sam's arm towards his own body, while Sam exerted all his strength towards the counter. After another three or four minutes of strenuous exertion, their arms were no longer vertical, but despite Sam's effort both arms were now close to Eddie's body, giving him a distinct advantage in leverage. As Eddie smiled and sighed with the effort of holding Sam, the big man groaned as his strength gave out and his arm was flattened to the outer edge of the counter. As the crowd roared their approval, Sam shook Eddie's hand but seemed too dumbfounded to comment on what had happened. Eddie suggested that although Sam's arms were probably stronger than his, there was the possibility that fingers and wrists played a more important part. Sam dismissed the suggestion, adding he was sure that Eddie's fingers were no stronger than his.

To prove his point he asked the proprietor if he would sell him a new pack of cards. Like any good landlord, Mr Horsburgh donated a new pack of cards without charge. Flipping the cards rapidly, Sam demonstrated that it was his intention to tear the fifty-two cards in half. Then, bunching them back, he gripped them tightly and pressing inwards with his wrists moving slowly in a wringing motion, he sheared the cards in half. Handing one half to Eddie, he suggested he had proved his point that it was not finger or wrist strength that had determined the outcome of their hand or arm wrestling competition. Eddie, blithe as usual, shrugged his shoulders and Sam, anxious to resolve the matter, asked Eddie to show what he could do with a new pack of cards.

The smile on Eddie's face disturbed Sam somewhat, as it did the audience in the Merchant's Arms. No one could be quite sure what would happen when he was around. But the mood changed when he insisted that to destroy another pack of cards was unnecessary. Would there be any objection, he asked, if he took one of the halved packs and tore it in two? The buzz of expectancy became a clamour for action as the crowd roared their approval. Accepting their mandate, Eddie took centre stage, asking that the half pack be examined before he commenced. Rolling up his sleeves he asked them to observe that what he was about to do was real and not a conjuring trick. Gripping the half pack in one hand, he showed them that there was only space for three fingers, then taking a grip with the other hand he signalled he was ready for the difficult task. Using the same technique as Sam, he pressed inwards and started to 'wring', but seconds later it seemed he had made little progress. The young men shouted encouragingly while the older generation appealed for silence, feeling that Eddie would succeed if left to concentrate. There was an eerie hush as Eddie concentrated. They could see he was having difficulty in holding his grip on such a small surface. There was a deep sigh as his hands came apart, his arms shot up in the air and his smile returned. He walked over to the counter, opened his hands and two quarters of the original pack spilled out.

I thanked Sam junior for telling me about the contest, but asked him now to be kind enough to shed light on the significance of the box. The younger man looked at Bill and Ben for approval before continuing. It appeared that Eddie had asked Sam over to a table for a private discussion. He had told Sam that during his sailing days he had won many arm-wrestling contests, some of them against men heavier than Sam. When he thought the odds were weighted too heavily against him, he had contrived to make the match at the counter as opposed to a table. He had always positioned himself with his back to the counter, which enabled him to hold and ultimately pull, whereas his opponent had to push away from his own body and source of strength. He had stressed to Sam that muscles do not push, they pull. Sam had been so impressed by Eddie's frankness and honesty that he had decided to demonstrate his gratitude in some tangible form. The end result was the glass box, on the base of which rested two quarters of the torn pack, with the name 'Sorenson 1' and the half pack, 'Sampson 2'. Originally there had been a small brass plate indicating the date of the contest.

It was only idle curiosity on my part, but I thought fit to ask the date. When Sam's son informed me that the contest had taken place on the 25 July, 1914, I could only smile, knowing it would certainly be impolite to divulge it to the old author. As I neared the end of my report, I could see that reminiscing was top priority in the mind of the old chap. He had listened all the way through, invariably smiling and from time to time coughing as the moisture in his eyes glistened. 'You are a remarkable man, Mr Ling,' he said, 'but how could it be otherwise with a name like Wil Ling?' Accepting his compliment, I told him it had been a pleasure to have satisfied him; it had always been my aim to seek out the truth. As an investigative journalist, my life had too often been threatened when my reports exposed some corrupt politician or unscrupulous business tycoon. It was good fortune that this time I was reporting back on a man who had made many people happy. As he looked earnestly at me, I concluded my report: 'Mr Sorenson, your father was a well respected and very popular man; he was one of Leith's characters.'

The old author smiled his appreciation and, after confirming some of the details, asked in a rather facile fashion whether I had noted the date of the contest between Sampson and Sorenson. I reacted in a similar vein, asking him to give me a date and, if correct, I would be pleased to confirm it. He burst out laughing, then, looking tentatively at me, he quoted: '25 July, 1914'. 'Correct,' I replied, 'and remember, Mr Sorenson, that you are the one who on this occasion used that awesome number; you may recollect I promised not to mention it again.' The old author apologised. 'I'm sorry I was so irritable a short time ago, but I felt your investigation was becoming too intrusive, particularly as far as my family was concerned. However, the end result has been exciting and most enjoyable; you may have boosted my faith in the better aspects of human nature.'

I took the opportunity to emphasise why my visits to Grangemouth and Leith had been necessary. It was only after my journey to Kerryville in the States that I knew Chancitt had been a real person. I discovered that he was more obnoxious and dangerous than the character in the novel. From Kerryville to Colombia he had left many victims as he 'snaked' along. By the time he reached South America, he was no longer a 'snake in the grass' – more a vulture feeding voraciously on the cocaine-contaminated remnants of society. Having served his apprenticeship, he had now soared high in the criminal calendar and achieved his target of illicitly supplying cocaine on a wholesale basis. Once he teamed up with Pierre le Blanc, their illicit stills had turned out enough cocaine to supply a continent of addicts.

As I followed their trail through Colombia, I saw many examples of cocaine poisoning, and although I knew that Chancitt was only one of many plying their deadly product, I cursed his short stay in our mortal coil. When I reached the village where Chanceet had been born, I was pleasantly surprised that over a few years he had been able to rescue his people from the thraldom of the cocaine barons and organise and restructure their agricultural policy, concentrating on feeding the people and placing the coca plant low on the agenda. When I saw what Chanceet had achieved, I knew I should do what I could to publicise the dangers of cocaine addiction. Having trailed Chancitt as far as his death bed in the North of England, I knew my quest was drawing to an end. However, I still attached importance to the thrashing of Lucius Chancitt by the seaman Sorenson in a South American inn and felt it should be investigated before I closed the case. As seaman Sorenson was no longer alive, the only source available to me were Sorenson's friends or their descendants on the East Coast of Scotland.

At this point the author could no longer suppress his emotion and almost shouted: 'And what did you discover, Mr Ling?' I asked him to sit back and relax and I would do my best to report verbatim what transpired. 'As I have already made clear, Mr Sorenson, your father was a very popular and talented man; his wisdom was ahead of his years. Within a short time he was recognised as a character dispensing wisdom and fun, often at the same time. The old man Ben told me of an occasion when some of the 'young fry' were boasting of their sexual maturity and ability to acquire drugs that gave them a 'kick'. Nobody had paid too much attention, but Eddie, feeling the urge to educate, had drawn them aside. It appears, Mr Sorenson, that your father, a born salesman, had decided to teach them a lesson. They listened attentively, knowing that your father was no fool, but towards the end, a rather highly strung nineteen-year-old boasted he knew methods whereby he could protect himself against venereal infection. When your father asked him if he could guarantee that he would not infect the prostitute, the abashed young man was dumbstruck and before he could reply, your father told him there was no natural law which indicated that man was superior to woman. He then asked what his attitude would be if he discovered that his mother had at some time been a prostitute. It was a very thoughtful young man who left the pub that night.

The next subject on the agenda was drugs and their abuse, particularly the lethal effects of cocaine addiction. He painted a lurid picture of what had happened to some of his shipmates who had been inveigled into using cocaine, how they had become addicted and the agony they suffered before dying. He told them of an experience inside an American waterside inn. A rather hook-nosed, swarthy individual had approached him and offered to sell him a 'fix', the name Americans used for illicit drugs. When he knew he was being offered cocaine, he told the pedlar to get lost. An argument developed and a fight took place, with the pedlar ending up unconscious on the floor. Your father confessed that had his shipmates not intervened and restrained him, he would have killed the pedlar. He told the young men he had acted foolishly; his emotions had overcome his common sense. If he had killed the pedlar, there was always another rogue or idiot to take his place. He should have done his best to show the pedlar the error of his ways, as only by education would the curse of addiction be conquered.

It was only natural that the young men wanted to know more regarding the fight that had taken place. Your father took them to task for being too bloodthirsty; he had no intention of embellishing an incident he would rather forget. After all, he had only told them the story to show that however well-intentioned a person might be, the brain should always dominate the fist. It was typical of your father that he asked them at the end of his lecture whether they had absorbed his message regarding the importance of education. 'I trust, gentlemen, that you have all listened carefully and now realise the benefit of further education. To sum up, be kind and considerate to women, knowing they are the equal partners of men and should be treated as such. Remember true love can exist without sex, but those who seek sex as a pathway to love often find disappointment, disillusion and despair. Regarding the dope pedlar, take my advice and say no. If you accept my viewpoint and wish to contribute to a better and safer society, then off to the local library to learn what you can about addictive drugs like cocaine and how, when abused, it can cause serious illness, often malfunction of the nervous system, in which the victim suffers hallucinations and has visions of being in heaven, but invariably ends languishing in hell. If he persists in "fixing" his appointment with heaven, he will only expedite his descent into the nether regions. His last few months on earth will be spent as a pain-racked, slobbering idiot, dying from the effects of cocaine poisoning. Once you have learned, through your books, gentlemen, of the seriousness of drug addiction and feel you wish to spread the gospel, then come back and see me and we will discuss how it could be done.'

It was at this point that I had asked Bill how he could remember the quaint wording of Eddie's lecture to the young men. Old Bill, now nearing his century, admitted that although his memory was far from perfect, he still remembered the speech almost word for word. 'You see,' he said, 'I was that clever nineteen-year-old who thought he knew everything. Eddie changed all that and I never forgot him.'

The old author's eyes were misting over again, his voice was husky as he told me that he had always associated his father with fun and games. 'I'm sure,' he said, 'old Bill would not be far off the mark concerning the language my father would use when lecturing the young men. I know he was an excellent linguist and as a salesman he would have been capable of choosing words that would convey his message in an orthodox but interesting fashion. He was considered by many to be a bit of a wag.' As I nodded agreement he suddenly asked: 'Was Chancitt's name ever mentioned?' As I shook my head, I made him aware of his father's steadfastness when the occasion demanded it. The young men had been too curious and frivolous regarding minor details. His father had taken them to task and told them in no uncertain manner that the purpose of the story was not to entertain, but to enlighten them concerning the deadly danger of drug addiction.

His look of wonderment was such that I felt compelled to clarify. 'The name of Chancitt was never mentioned.' For a moment he seemed mystified before replying, 'What I cannot understand, Mr Ling, is why he did not link Lucius Chancitt with drug-smuggling when lecturing the young men.' Never one to encourage a mystery when a down-to-earth explanation is available, I expanded a little. 'Your father, Mr Sorenson, was not only a well-loved character, he was also a gentleman in the best sense of the word. He was kind and considerate, also chivalrous and, although endowed with above-average strength, was gentle unless aroused by some injustice or injury to himself or his fellow men. When addressing the young men, he was in the main concerned with principles and ethics, as opposed to principals and personalities. Being an honest salesman, he stuck to his principles and achieved his target.'

As he pondered my statement, I continued: 'It was, I believe, as you were approaching your teens that your father, for economic reasons, decided to go back to sea. Knowing you had mastered the *modus operandi* of the 'birds and the bees', he was nevertheless concerned and felt the necessity of educating you, before his departure, in the hazards and danger to health of smoking and drinking. You had already been briefed regarding proper conduct towards women, but had now reached the stage where he felt it essential to warn you that prostitutes were off limit and any dipping around in that area would be asking for trouble and end in disaster. It was, however, the effects of drug addiction that predominated in the mind of your father. When he addressed the young men, he saw no need to mention names and divert attention, rather concentrating on his message, but as this time it was *you*, his *son*, he felt you should know the whole truth. From reading your novel, Mr Sorenson, I would say he did an excellent job!'

The old man seemed lost for words as he sat back in his chair, his hand covering his mouth and chin. Then looking up as if contemplating his answer, he smiled graciously towards me and gave his verdict. 'You're a wonderful man, Mr Ling. I know now how observant, patient and kind you can be. I must apologise for considering your investigation into our family history as having been unnecessary and irksome. I can see now the necessity for an investigation to explore every channel before giving an assessment.' As I thanked him for his kind words, he waved his hand and asked leave to proceed. There was a grin on his face as he restarted: 'What I was coming to was your advent into that rather nebulous sphere of numerology and my feeling that it should not be entirely discounted. You referred to my father's instructions when I was approaching my teens. In fact the day he gave me his instructions was the 25 July, 1926.' Diplomatically inclined, I made no comment, but the excited old man pointed out: 'Don't you see, Mr Ling, I was thirteen years old that day. Now I am not superstitious but it does make you think.'

This, I thought, was the appropriate moment for my confession. 'I do agree, Mr Sorenson, we are all rather apt when mystified to use the word coincidence, even concurrence is used, and as you know, "con" signifies the prefix "with". Now I think I am as much "with it" as anyone and prepared to go with the current, but it is the way the current is running that disturbs me.' The old man seemed prepared for a little nonsense and replied accordingly. 'You are like my father, Mr Ling, a bit of a wag, but do carry on.'

'Your family, Mr Sorenson, have from time to time been associated with the twenty-fifth of July. I must now tell you that I was born on the twenty-fifth of July, 1939.' Quick as a flash the old man interjected: No wonder you were concerned at the way the current was running. A little more than a month later the

103

Second World War started.' I could have been churlish and reminded him that the First World War started not long after he was born in 1913, but consoled him with the close proximity of his thirteenth birthday and the National Strike in 1926.

He laughed and clapped me on the shoulder. 'Touché,' he said, and then proceeded to tell me what he thought of numerology. 'I'm sure you were to some extent being facetious when you indicated that it was a product of the occult and that only the high priests knew its secrets. Without being too enigmatic, I trust you might agree that the original organisation would be well past its "sell-by date". If they ever did exist, I would imagine they would, in this fast-moving world of ours, have already instituted the new religion of computerology.' I was surprised at his radical approach and attempted to join in, but he would have none of it, indicating he had more to say. 'I was a bit rash in giving all the mystics the credit of being religious affiliates. Too often many of them are confidence tricksters and scoundrels enriching themselves at the expense of the poor and credulous. There may be some who, having no religion of their own, do attempt to commune with God. I cannot claim to be religious, but I do respect the sincere believer who is prepared to die for his belief and I have nothing but contempt for the bigot who uses his religion as an excuse for destroying his fellow man.'

Before he could gather his thoughts, I reminded him of his suggestion that the material I had already given him could possibly be used as the basis of a successful novel. Unashamedly I referred to his father's influence on his way of thinking. 'Your father was a wonderful man, obviously ahead of his time and recognised as a champion of the underdog.' The old author, although impressed, wanted time to think. 'Take it easy, Mr Ling,' he said, 'you are correct, but remember you are younger than I am and I still adhere to the old adage, "Look before you leap"!' I told him I was sorry for rushing things, but felt an urge to publicise the good work of Chanceet, admitting that the fact that he had saved my life played a significant part in my desire for speed. The old man appeared to be considering the viability of a message-provoking novel. Some seconds later I interjected: 'It was your character Lucius Chancitt that sent me halfway round the world. At that time I felt it highly improbable that the monster you depicted could have existed in real life. I know now it was Chanceet, submerged in my subconscious, that sent me forth to trail his miserable father.'

The old man laughed and slapped the table. 'Bravo, Mr Ling. As a master of drama, I am sure your novel will be a great success.' Taken aback, I was dumbstruck for a moment but managed to assert that if I had to, I would certainly try, but felt that the subject really merited the attention of a master craftsman.

He responded quickly. 'Your flattery is noted, Mr Ling, but not required. I know full well you would do your best, but after all, it was my father who recognised the evil in Chancitt and consistently attempted to influence his fellow men against the evils of drug taking.'

By the end of the afternoon Sorenson had decided he would attempt to create a readable and exciting novel that would not only entertain but also serve to shock the public into realising the dangers and misery they should expect if they allowed themselves to be enticed into drug taking. Handing over the material in my possession, I promised to assist him with any research or detective work that might be required. Having made up his mind, he was a happy man and raring to go. 'Well, Mr Ling, despite the time we may have wasted airing our views on mystics and religion, I feel we are now on the track of something creative. I would not expect "25" to rear its head again.'

Having completed our business, I made for the door but before I could exit, the phone rang and an excited Sorenson asked me to wait. Whatever the message, he was happy and wanted me to share it. He signalled me to be seated and, as the conversation continued, he became more and more excited. It appeared that congratulations were on an ascending scale. There was a big beaming smile on his face as he told me that his grandson's wife had given birth to a boy late on the previous evening. 'It's my first great-grandchild, Mr Ling.' As I congratulated him, I noticed the date on his rather ornate desk calendar. I drew his attention to the vivid red numerals. 'Apart from my great-grandchild, what is so important about the 26th of April?' I must have appeared smug as I replied, 'Nothing in particular, but remember last night was the 25th.' Mr Sorenson is a big man and when he laughs, furniture and anything not fixed to the floor tends to rumble. I know very little about shock waves or the Richter scale but I'm sure the reading would have been quite impressive. In between his gales of laughter he embraced me, then pushing me out into the hallway, he almost shouted, 'Be off, before I have you shot, and never mention that number again.'

CHAPTER 8

My sabbatical well and truly over, I returned to my desk at the *Morning Sun*. My editor greeted me in his usual comradely style: 'Where the hell have you been, Mr Ling?' Being a resourceful person, I made him aware of my adventures in South America, knowing full well he had received my original despatches. Looking over his spectacles while chewing his teeth, he almost snarled back: 'You know what I mean, Mr "Not-so-Willing".' I smiled sweetly back but demanded to know for what crime I was being punished. To my surprise he made no effort to indulge in verbal fencing, a clear indication that he was indeed a very worried man. He gave me a wry smile and put me in the picture. 'I expected you back about a week ago, Wil. I'm in trouble and require the services of a wily and resourceful correspondent.'

It transpired that during my absence the paper had lost two of its brightest young reporters. One had been hospitalised and it was feared he had not long to live, while the other had been stabbed to death in the hallway of a Mayfair flat. Although the flat was occupied by a highly respected business man, the police thought fit to investigate his connections with a rather shady South American pharmaceutical company. It appeared the police and customs had reason to believe that the young man's death was due to his investigations into illicit drug trafficking. 'See what you can do, Wil,' he said, 'I don't expect miracles, but drugs are high on the agenda and while you're at it a little footage on the political front won't go wrong; the stupidity and lack of humanity of the present government is always good copy.'

I knew how he felt and tried to placate him, but he insisted on finishing his piece. 'Since this lot came in, greed has been the password. They couldn't run a sweet shop, let alone govern a nation. We have only ourselves to blame; we are the fools who allowed these idiots to manipulate us.' Knowing my editor was a case-hardened newspaper man, I was surprised and marvelled at his intense feelings against the present régime. I could only assume that he thought they were moribund zombies controlled by some evil power. I knew this to be rather far-fetched, but after a spell of scouting around, I wondered if there was some element of truth in my original assumption. Despite my reputation in the corridors of power and big business, I had always managed in the past to extract information from some underpaid or like-minded civil servant. Although the information was invariably minimal, my powers of deduction and subsequent investigation often allowed me to unravel certain factors in common to reveal a web of intrigue. Now, however, my potential contacts were deadpan faces seeming to be programmed by a computer in need of repair.

Wil Ling by name and willing by nature, I stuck to the job in hand, managing to break into the code and resuscitate one of the rebel morons. It took a goodly number of drinks before he would converse like a normal adult. I can only assume the alcohol acted like an anaesthetic, allowing him to speak without fear. I was patient and kind and he rewarded me with information that proved useful during my night school activities. Originally a civil servant, he was now a clerk in a company that specialised in 'privateering' national assets. He admitted his lifestyle had changed somewhat. Everything was 'go' now. No one reached their target and most were unaware of the ultimate destination. But his boss was doing well, having just matriculated to the 'College of Million Pound Chairmen'. Although my friend believed in private enterprise, he was not amused, Why was it after the transition that his salary was still much the same, while his new boss had thought fit to award himself one million pounds a year? It was obviously a heart-rending experience for my new-found friend, so I sympathised with the disgruntled chief clerk.

Knowing he had passed his advanced accountancy exams, I felt he should be given enough time to air his views on the intricacies of financial deals and how they affected the public at large. Like all good newspaper men, I will not reveal the name of the man I questioned, but I thought fit to ask my editor to arrange a meeting with the Chairman, on the basis that the public would be interested in learning something of the lifestyle and the aspirations of a prominent 'captain of industry'. My editor gave me a queer look, but I assured him I would behave myself and return with a story suitable for publication, the contents of which would be agreed upon by the Chairman and myself. My editor agreed to try and arrange the meeting and I added that if the Chairman let slip in his demeanour some indication of liaison with shysters or members of the nether world, I would take note and feel free to proceed, when appropriate, to expose him. He shook his head before warning me: 'Take it easy, Wil, I'd hate to lose you.'

The Chairman was a cheery man; at least he was at the beginning of the interview. I complimented him on being a high flyer in the million pound stakes and asked if it had in any way altered his life. He seemed quite frank, assuring me he was still a keen fisherman, played cricket for the village team and was also a church elder. He admitted his increase in salary had allowed him to fish in deeper waters; he had been able to spend a considerable part of his increase in salary on a modern yacht and was rapidly becoming, according to some new friends, a skilled yachtsman. On cue I asked: 'So you might say your tenfold increase in salary has to some extent altered your attitude to life?'

109

He snapped back: 'If you mean, Ling, do I snub my old friends, the answer is definitely, no!' I dismissed his lack of the title 'Mister' and answered him properly. 'Mr Goldstock, my function is just to interview an extremely successful businessman and do it in such a way that the public are made aware of the advantages of becoming rich, but they should also be able to appreciate the stress and anxiety it can mean if handled improperly. You have nothing to fear in being frank, and you can vet our conversation before it is published. For that matter, you can tell me to leave now.' He gave a wan smile and asked me to proceed. 'Your company employs many thousands of workers, their take-home pay has remained static while your salary has increased enormously. What is your answer to those who consider this to be most unfair?' He smirked as he replied: 'I would sympathise with them, but tell them we are all paid at the rate for the job.'

As he looked questioningly at me, I told him that if I was a worker or member of his staff his reply would certainly not assuage me. For a fleeting moment his disdainful look betrayed his inner thoughts, but he quickly recovered and, putting on a serious face, trusted I would understand. 'I would tell them that my responsibility as Chairman is to ensure that any judgements or decisions I make will benefit the company and its shareholders and remind them that many of them are workers within the company. I am paid one million pounds per year for my special skills and financial knowledge. A mistake could be measured in millions but fortunately our profit level remains high and continues to rise.' Recognising his heavy responsibility, I suggested that in such circumstances there had to be rules or a code of practice. He agreed his position was an onerous one; there had to be constant contact with the banks, DTI and certain other government agencies. A strict code of practice was laid down and it was his responsibility to ensure it was adhered to. Regarding the code of practice, I asked what his view was concerning someone defaulting and thus cheating the public at large. It was obvious from the way he reacted that I had hit a raw nerve and I entered a minus in my memory bank. I referred to the tragic drowning of Sir Ilka Mair, who had been charged with embezzlement. I could see his fingers trembling but he retained his facial composure and huskily replied, as I expected: 'Ilka was wrong in what he did, however I think you will realise that you cannot quote me on that sad event.' I nodded agreement, read to him my report of the interview and asked if he would agree to publication. He seemed relieved, even pleased, and quipped: 'I trust from what I hear the public will realise I am human after all, that I'm just one of them.'

As I thanked him for the interview, he patted my shoulder and gripped my right hand, then bringing his left hand down he encompassed my hand between his. It was a most peculiar handshake, his right hand was firm while his left hand seemed intent on soothing me. As his fingers moved towards my wrist, I felt as if they were tapping a message. Having led a healthy life, I know little of the messages transmitted in the nether world and could not be expected to know if the content was masonic or messianic. Having learned enough, I gripped tightly and he relinquished his hold. As he did so, he thought fit to praise me for being a journalist of exceptional character. Although I was now convinced he was a 'fiddler', I knew I had no time to pursue the tune he had in mind, noted the impression of his behaviour and notched it up for future reference. I made a point of returning to the chief clerk, assuring him that the information he had given me was accurate and sympathising with his invidious position. We agreed to help each other in the future. Any information I received would be from an anonymous source, while articles from my pen would expose the arrogance and greed of the new type of company chairmen who fleeced the public while treating their clerks as disposable salary slaves.

It was indeed a happy and useful relationship, particularly when colleagues of the chief clerk discovered they could air their views without fear of victimisation, while I could investigate further and hopefully provide the ammunition, should some sticky-fingered city gent be stealing too much from the public purse. It is not my intention to bore you with the results of enforced privatisation of the nation's assets; most of us know that privateering would be a more apt and honest description. When arrogance and greed dominate, it is inevitable that accountability, responsibility and consideration of one's fellow man are booted out of the window.

My liaison with the clerks soon gave me a workload far greater than I had expected. The ill-thought-out policies of the government, exacerbated by the idiotic ineptitude of the departmental 'yes men', had seen to that. It was a frustrating period. Although I had managed to collect evidence that would have put a worker in jail immediately and for a long stretch, I had to suffer the agony of seeing upper crust criminals bailed out by their highly paid lawyers, who by procrastination and clever use of our property 'weighted' laws, were able to keep their clients in opulent sanctuary. How I longed for a modern legal system in which people would supersede property! However, knowing that it would take longer than a weekend to change our archaic legal system, I decided to concentrate on more urgent matters.

I thought of Chanceet and his fight against the cocaine barons and wondered what stage the old author had reached in his proposed novel. My editor must have had similar thoughts when he asked me to discuss future policy. He came straight to the point: 'I remember telling you, Wil, that while some articles exposing government "cock ups" would be acceptable, I did ask you to concentrate on the drug scene. You can forget the sordid state of government, at least for the time being, and get cracking

112

on helping the police and customs in their fight against the drug dealers.' I felt abashed, wondering what he was up to. His reference to the young reporter who had lost his life in the Mayfair flat led me to apologise for not having done enough in helping the police trace the killer. He barely heard my apology since he was so intent on outlining his plan. It was his intention to make full use of the front page of the paper. The police and customs would be invited to give their views on how the public could help in eradicating the drug menace. When he removed his spectacles and looked fixedly in my direction, I knew I had to pay special attention or I would be blasted. 'You will work in close liaison with customs and excise. With your experience in South America and of British ports on how the drug smugglers operate, you are obviously the best man to represent the paper.' As I nodded mechanically, he gave me an evil smile, replaced his spectacles and assured me, 'You see, Wil, yon time you decided on a wee holiday you concentrated your attention on how these bloody rascals operate.' My editor, a shrewd Scot, knew how I would react. Having referred to the increased death toll of drug addicts, he emphasised in particular the deaths of three wee bairns and had me so incensed that I felt like leaving immediately, seeking out the culprits and personally strangling them on the spot. My editor shook me by the hand, wished me good fortune and advised me to watch my back.

As far as I was concerned this was to be a crusade. I should have known better. Harking back to my engineering apprentice days, I should have remembered old Sandy's advice that the preparation for a job can be more arduous than the job itself. The police and customs were anxious to make use of any newspaper space that helped them in combating the activities of smugglers, but first and foremost extra manpower was essential. The government's policy of deregulation and skimping on resources should be exposed, and if I could help, they would be grateful.

A Chief Officer of Customs put it succinctly: 'Tell this *******
government to pull its finger out and give me double the number
of "snifters" we have at present, and I guarantee we will manage
something really worthwhile.' I laid myself open to a measure of
friendly banter when I asked if doubling the number of drug
dogs would make a significant contribution. His reply was, to
say the least, educational. 'Extra dogs would be helpful, Mr Ling,
but I'm referring to 'seadogs', the human kind that can handle a
gun during an emergency.' Realising that this represented
preparation for the task in hand, I took his point and promised
to do my best in stressing his requirement through the newspaper.
I also asked that at some time in the future I should be allowed to
keep in contact with them as they pursued their objective. His
comment was fair enough: 'If you can show me that you are
helping us, then you can rest assured you will be welcome
aboard.'

For a full month I made forays in the direction of the
'Gasworks' and buttonholed as many members of Parliament as
possible, concentrating on those whose constituencies were
coastal and particularly those with ports. I achieved a moderate
degree of success by putting it to them that my earlier questioning
of their constituents had shown that the people were concerned
and alarmed by the increase in crime, connecting much of it with
unemployment and drug addiction. Now, however, the
Government's failure to control drug smuggling had become a
national scandal. Now that young people were becoming
enmeshed and dying, it would not be long before the people
would feel forced to oust the Government unless it took
immediate action and provided the resources to forestall a major
tragedy. Some of the 'coastal' MPs hummed and hawed, but after
a bit of 'politicking' and my assurance that I, as an honest reporter,
would inform their constituents of their opinion, they asked for
a parley. Knowing that the credence and credit of the Government

114

was at zero and that their jobs were in jeopardy, they gave me statements that were acceptable and attuned to their survival. Whether my intervention played a significant part or not is not for me to say, but, be that as it may, the Chief Officer of Customs must have sensed a measurable degree of advancement when he welcomed me 'aboard'.

I set to with a will and although I managed to acquire information that put a few miserable drug traffickers and minor criminals behind bars, I felt that I was only scratching the surface of the drug problem. In between times I wrote to Mr Sorenson about the stage he had reached with his novel, hoping he would let slip some ideas that might help me in my investigations. His cheerful assertion that the novel was coming along fine but it would be some time before it would be completed did nothing for my morale. Why were things going so slowly, or was it that in my impatient state I was travelling too fast to recognise vital clues? In a state of pique, I asked the literary correspondent on the paper how long it normally took to write a novel. He looked at me wonderingly before replying, 'Anything between twenty days and twenty years and the time factor does not guarantee success.' I felt so frustrated that I immediately departed, making a beeline for the nearest hostelry in which to drown my sorrows.

You may not believe this, but in the morning I felt cold sober and I welcomed the 'shun that sawn' so brightly in the sky. Three tomato juices later, topped up with Worcester Sauce, I was even more sober and could almost think clearly. Collecting my mail from behind the front door, I made straight for my desk and sat down . . . carefully.

CHAPTER 9

As a columnist I am used to receiving scurrilous letters, particularly from Tory backwoodsmen. Opening my mail cautiously, I separated the wheat from those that were chaffing me and then got down to business. By a stroke of good fortune I had been assigned the reporting of a rather special meeting between British and Brazilian business men. It was considered important enough for the Government to have arranged the venue and necessary security. The press corps were given appropriate passes and, being one of that select group, I looked forward to learning something. If, on the other hand, it lacked interest, I could always snooze through it and collect my stereotyped report in the late afternoon. Little did I know that the next twenty-four hours would be fast moving, exciting and a little dangerous.

The head of the Brazilian delegation was a well-known tycoon, a portly man, whose golden teeth glittered as the cameras flashed. He spoke through an interpreter, outlining the general plan he had in mind. After his speech there was the usual polite clapping, more I suspect for his golden molar display than for the questionable contents of his script. I wakened up in time to see the star performer of the show. He was a handsome Brazilian, in his forties, I guessed, but it was not his speech in perfect English that captivated me; it was his appearance that sent a shiver down my spine.

As my mind flashed back to a bedroom in downtown Montevideo, my hand involuntarily caressed the five-inch scar at the back of my head. The man on the platform bore a striking resemblance to a member of the Uruguayan diplomatic service. I had known him as Jehu Cristo and, suspecting him of cocaine smuggling, I had been tracking him in that city. He had entered a rather sleazy hotel and I had, as I thought, melted into the background. A quarter of an hour later he emerged and boarded a taxi. By various devices I managed to gain access to the room he had occupied and was patiently surveying his possessions. The thump on the back of my head stopped all that and when I came back to life, I found myself trussed up in a blanket. Although my pride was hurt more than my head, I knew I had to extricate myself quietly and prepare to fight for my life. It seemed an inordinately long time before I could free myself and crawl silently to a shaft of light shining from the adjoining room. From my worm's eye view I could see Jehu Cristo rifling through papers and stuffing them in a briefcase, then putting his hands underneath the drawer of a bureau he brought forth a package. Although I was almost erect, I decided to play possum and conserve my energy for what might become a fight for survival. A minute later he was gone and shortly afterwards I made an ignominious exit. My feeling of humiliation changed to one of extraordinary relief when I was only fifty yards away from the hotel. There was an almighty explosion and all the windows blew out, a clear indication that the 'big boys' thought I was too nosey.

If the man on the platform was indeed Jehu Cristo, then I owed him one. I made a point of contacting an attendant favourable to my cause and questioned him concerning the handsome one. Yes, the man on the platform was the top diplomatic member of the Brazilian delegation and his name was Jehu Cristo. I told him I was extremely interested and it was my intention to seek the autograph of the diplomat, but preferably somewhere in private. He looked me straight in the eye, tapped his nose and, being a true friend, gave me all the information I required. After the

117

meeting, Jehu Cristo would remain in London as the Vice Ambassador of Brazil and in two months would probably replace the present Ambassador who was due to retire. The word 'vice' and the irony of the situation must have been reflected on my face for my friend thought fit to express himself. 'Good luck to you, pal. See you get the b-----d.' I knew now that I was on to something really big. I also knew it could be extremely dangerous, particularly if I allowed the scar on my head to dictate my actions. I decided it was now or never if I was to play a significant part in the fight against drug addiction, but it could mean 'finito' if caught by the drug smugglers and an unwanted 'middle aged stretch' if caught by our own police. However, if successful, I could be instrumental in putting a number of millionaire drug traffickers into solitary confinement, with the keys mysteriously disappearing.

I booked into the hotel where the delegation was staying and asked to see the manager. I told him of my close relationship with Mr Jehu Cristo and asked if it would be possible to give me a room on the same landing. As he demurred, I agreed he had to be careful, but it was a pity as I had envisaged giving a champagne supper to enable us to re-live old memories. When I told him that to have to traipse through the hotel was really not on, a miraculous change took place. I would not say he was too obsequious in manner, but definitely greedy when I heard what a champagne supper would cost. An arrangement was made whereby I could occupy a room immediately opposite Mr Jehu Cristo. His number was 199 and mine 169.

As I sat in the foyer planning my programme for the afternoon, the porter asked if he should take my bag upstairs. I declined, telling him that I had important papers I intended to peruse. I had no intention of risking someone discovering what was in my bag of tricks. Ordering a drink, I sat back and watched the world go by. Half an hour later, while a group of Americans and other colonials were cluttering the ground in the front of reception, I ascended to the first floor and deposited my bag in my official room. Everything seemed to be in tune and even the numbers were helpful. Being an ex-scout, I had come prepared. Opening the appropriate blade, I unscrewed the number six and turned it round so that my room number was now 199. Being an accommodating kind of person, I did the reverse on the Cristo apartment. Downstairs the Americans were still milling around and another care-worn receptionist had taken over. In the melée I chanced my luck and asked for 199. As he handed over the appropriate piece of plastic they use these days, he muttered 'Cristo'.

Being suddenly hard of hearing, I nodded and sympathised with him. After all, it must be irksome to have to remain calm when so many people demand attention. With my 199 card I entered the new 169, knowing that if caught I could claim to have been made the victim of a practical joke. But just in case some intelligent janitor realised what had happened and tried to enter the room, I wedged the door, knowing that I could kick it free if required. For a full hour I searched but could find no incriminating evidence. Then I remembered my 'worm's eye' view in Uruguay. I had already looked through four drawers of a rather massive bureau but had been unsuccessful. Removing the first two drawers, I found nothing sticking to the bottom. It was a case of 'third time lucky'. I could feel what could be a thin parcel of foolscap taped to the base of the drawer. From then on it was an extremely nerve-racking business, wondering if I could manage to photograph in time what amounted to political dynamite. It was the plans and directives of a criminal drug cartel. I knew that if caught in the act, I could expect to be shot by one of their hired assassins.

It took under half an hour to copy the documents but it felt like hours. With nervous hands I assembled them in proper order and re-taped them to the underside of the drawer. Realising the importance of evidence, I photographed a number of items in the room, even a close-up of part of a quotation notched by some vandal on the front of the bureau. It read 'Honi soit qui mal y—?' Ensuring that everything was left as I found it, I moved over to my room, satisfied that what was in my possession could be extremely valuable in the fight against international drug trafficking. I telephoned CID and asked for Donald Mackenzie. 'Big Mac' was not available, the young lady told me, he was out on a case but would I like to leave a message.

'Yes,' I said, 'tell him that Wil Ling has just phoned and has information regarding a shipment of cocaine. His immediate presence is required if the criminals are to be caught.' Leaving the name of the hotel and my room number, I sat back and perused the copied documents. It was time for readjustment and I had just managed to change the room numbers back again when Big Mac burst in. 'And where are these criminals?' he asked. I felt quite proud of myself when I showed him the copied documents and told him how I had acquired them. 'What you have done is illegal. Do you think you can do just as you like?' His West Highland accent did not comfort me but neither did I allow it to deter me. 'Read the stuff, Mac, before you pass an opinion.' Big Mac put on his spectacles and got down to business. After a period of brow-furrowing, teeth-sucking and head scratching, he had made up his mind.

Looking over his specs at me he declaimed: 'Good Christ, Wil, this stuff is dynamite.' After assuring him that I had copied everything properly and replaced the evidence the way I found it, he advised that I should disappear and leave the rest to him. I agreed but asked to be kept informed. After all, I had the right to publish and that was my intention. As I volunteered to open up Room 199 and show him where to look for the documents, he looked at me in a fatherly fashion and asked for the card to Cristo's room. As I handed over the card, he revealed that the Secret Service would probably be in the room within the hour, but come what may he would see to it that I got my headline. I learned later that customs, the police and the security services can become entangled at times. Experts within the Home Office and the Foreign Office vied with each other concerning the best course of action to adopt. Despite this, an hour after I had left the hotel, special agents had secretly raided Room 199, and not long after, Mr Jehu Cristo had been escorted to a safe hiding hole where he was held incommunicado.

I certainly got my headlines, but the powers that be made me wait for them. What I had started ended with the exposure and imprisonment of several South American millionaires and their smuggling hirelings. The exposure highlighted the part that certain sections of big business were playing in the illicit drugs market. Over a two-week period more than a billion dollars of cocaine and similar substances were seized by the authorities. Jehu Cristo never achieved his ambassadorship. By a queer stroke of fate his dead body was discovered only yards from the Brazilian Embassy. It appeared that no one had even heard of him, nor had anyone heard the shot being fired. After all, in international circles the essence of diplomacy is to recognise that undue verbosity is most undignified.

Be that as it may, the paper's circulation increased dramatically and I earned the plaudits of my editor. What pleased me even more was a letter from old Mr Sorenson telling me it would not be long before his novel would be published. With letters passing between us, he was aware of the part I had played in the unmasking of the illicit drug millionaires. Knowing my love and respect for Chanceet, he was sure my hero would be very happy that the man whose life he had saved had to some degree repaid him by the elimination of some of his people's enemies. It was his intention to name his novel 'Chanceet' and he trusted I approved.

Editors are never satisfied. Only three weeks after our unusual scoop, mine suggested I should ease up a little on the drug scene and concentrate more on what he called the sleaze factor. I argued that from time immemorial corruption and bribery had been rife between government officials and their questionable friends. 'I know how you feel,' he said, 'but as from today you will concentrate on exposing the sleazy activities of certain ministers. Tomorrow you may well be back on your crusade against the drug barons. Meantime I have a newspaper to run and at present the man in the street has placed corruption and bribery on top of the agenda. It's as sleazy as that.'

Reluctantly accepting his directive, I asked for the file on the company chairman I had interviewed some time before. 'If you are referring to Goldstock, the Water Company Chairman, his dead body was recovered from a nearby reservoir at four o'clock this morning.' Noticing my incredulous look, he berated me for not being up to date with the latest headlines. I accepted I had a lot to learn, but reminded him that he, as editor, was responsible for headlines and I, a mere investigative journalist, was a collector of facts and evidence, too often concerned with the seamier side of life. He was not impressed. 'If you'll stop blethering, Wil, I'll put you in the picture.' It appeared that Mr Goldstock had become involved in an argument with customers who claimed his water was not only too dear but also very dirty. There had been a fracas and after the police had restored order, Mr Goldstock had taken centre stage and declared the only water he drank was the crystal clear water from his own works.

The derision that followed prompted Goldstock to say he was prepared to drink a glassful of the company water to prove it was not in any way contaminated. His challenge had been immediately accepted, there being ample supplies available. The leader of the consumer's delegation stepped forward and offered his sample, stressing that it had been taken from his kitchen tap only half an hour before. Having committed himself, the Chairman decided to make the most of a rather dicey situation. Holding up the sample, he argued: 'If I drink this man's sample it might satisfy him; on the other hand would it satisfy the rest of you?' As they murmured amongst themselves he continued: 'Surely a fairer method would be to mix all the samples together and allow me to drink a glassful of the mixture.' In full view of his audience he drank the mixture, commenting that it was a pleasure to drink the purest water in the land. He left in a dignified fashion and was never seen again. His body was discovered in a reservoir culvert four days later.

As I looked enquiringly at the editor, he shrugged his shoulders and told me that as far as the press was concerned, the body in the culvert had reached a 'dead end'. Suddenly I realised I had an interest. After all I had used the good services of my editor to engineer an interview with Mr Goldstock. Having studied the man at close range and evaluated his progress in business circles, I knew he was, or had been, a potential candidate for the ascending sleaze 'escalator'. My editor, the canny Scot that he was, was not forthcoming. 'Maybe aye and maybe no,' he said, 'but you are the investigator, I'm only the editor.' Dissatisfied with his attitude, but still curious to know why Fleet Street were treating it as a non-event, I decided to investigate.

I may never know what happened to the dead Chairman, for the following morning the editor conceded I had been right in forecasting coming events. Pointing to the paper's headline, 'Colombian Peasants Revolt', he told me my wish had come true and that he knew I would be only too pleased to report back on the struggle between the drug cartel and the peasants. Anticipating that the struggle could involve other South American States, he advised me that I should equip myself accordingly.

As I sat there looking out at the swirling December fog, I thought of warmer climes. The old rascal seemed to know what I was thinking and broke in on my reverie. 'Aye, Wil,' he said, 'you look after yourself. You could be in the Americas for quite some time. The cartel mainly involved in this dirty and dangerous business has interests as far as Key West in Florida.' It was the way he ended on a high note that convinced me he had read my mind. He knew that sooner or later I would, when circumstances permitted it, visit my cousin at his fruit farm. That afternoon, as I cleared my desk, I speculated on what to expect when taking up duty in South America. I had no illusions concerning the danger involved and knew I was no longer as physically fit as I had been on my SouthAmerican adventure some ten years before. This factor and the ratio of brawn to brain had to be recognised intelligently and even though I was wiser now, I still had to contend with the changes that had taken place.

Drug trafficking had changed dramatically, with modern methods of communication and transportation being used by those enemies of human society. Still, I admired my own particular cunning and felt exceeding pleased that I had copied for my own use the Cartel's documents and directives to Jehu Cristo and other agents. At least I had a good idea of how they operated. It was up to me to ensure that I remained anonymous for as long as possible. Have you ever experienced a situation where you feel that your life is a re-run of something that happened years before? I must admit that I had been at a farewell party with my friends the previous evening, but felt perfectly sober and knew that what was happening could only be described as uncanny. Having decided I deserved the day off, I shaved and dressed, then meandering lazily, I managed to make my way downstairs to the kitchen, switched on the percolator and proceeded to the living room. I heard the letter box pop as I drew the curtains and there it was, the *Morning Sun*. I must hasten to assure you that I am referring to my morning newspaper, not the golden orb in the sky, so rarely seen in fog-bound London.

The headline read: 'Author Hits Jackpot' and immediately below was a picture of the author Sorenson. Every detail seemed the same as three years ago. Suddenly I felt vulnerable. Was it a matter of mental transposition, or had some practical joker, with malice aforethought, pushed a three year-old newspaper through my letter box? My fingers trembled as I looked for the publication date, but the newspaper fell from my grasp when the door bell rang and the letter box flap rattled noisily. Cursing under my breath, I almost ran to the door. As I opened it and prepared to blast, I was taken aback by two smiling blue eyes and dulcet tones from ruby red lips as a beautiful young maiden announced herself. 'I'm Priscilla Pontefract, my employers Pringle and Pryce have instructed me to ensure that you receive this parcel. Inside you will find a letter of explanation.'

As I stood there, her maternal instincts took over. 'Are you all right, Mr Ling?' she enquired. 'Would you like to sit down somewhere?' Assuring her I was fit enough, but that I had been taken by surprise, she smiled acknowledgement and asked me to sign the acceptance note. As she left she wished me a Merry Christmas and I reciprocated. I waved to her just as she entered her car and she replied, in an idiom now universally accepted, 'Have a nice day'. Although curious to know what I had signed for, I still scuttled back to my newspaper. It was with relief I discovered that the paper and myself were within the same timescale. Sorenson had done it again. His new book, *Chanceet*, would be available to the public within a fortnight and was expected to be even more popular than *Sorenson*. Having co-operated with the author, I felt elated and welcomed his success, but felt rather peeved at not being made aware of potential publication. However, within myself I felt sure his new novel would help in the fight against drug trafficking. As I mused, I realised I had a parcel to open. My misgivings evaporated at a stroke as a copy of Sorenson's *Chanceet* was revealed and attached to it was a letter from the old author himself.

CHAPTER 10

I read the letter with great care, knowing it would be something rather special. It was dated 24th December, 1994, and read:-

'Dear Wil,

I have just heard from your editor that you will be departing to the Americas within a day or two. I would hazard a guess that you already know that our novel *Chanceet* has reached the stage of universal publication and the publishers feel it will be an outstanding success. It will be on sale to the public in a fortnight and knowing you would not be here, I have done a bit of arm-twisting and managed to have printed a full rough copy without frills. You will at least have with you the full story as you travel on what could be an enriching sabbatical, ending I trust in a successful crusade, together with *Chanceet*, against the evil power of the drug barons.'

I read his letter with mixed feelings. I was elated and proud that he should refer to the book as our novel but a little sad that I would not be with him at the official launch. There and then, I decided I would at least start reading his novel, but first I would read the newspaper credits. Although I knew the book was not a Christmas present, I felt sure he would have appreciated the irony of the situation. Being an agnostic like myself, he was irreligious but had already admitted a predisposition towards Christian ethics, believing that the man known as Christ was probably the first true communist on earth. Regarding the number '25', it had been a bone of contention on which we had all chewed in a civilised and human fashion. I could only hope it would not be too long before we were together again, enjoying the camaraderie of friends with a common aim.

Throwing aside the newspaper, I immersed myself in the novel, feeling sure I would be enjoying a unique experience. Regarding the characters, I was amused to see I had been cast as Will Light, and trusted I might not be short-circuited too early in the unfolding story. I should have known better for Sorenson had ensured that Will Light lived up to his name. He was a lovable person who shed light wherever he travelled, leaving felons panicking in his wake. Having supplied Sorenson with all the information I had gathered during my investigation of his villainous character, Lucius Chancitt, it was only natural I could expect to follow the story quickly. But I soon understood I was reading a masterpiece which merited my full consideration and my appreciation of a creative writer who believed ardently that his message would be universally accepted. I marvelled at his ability to change my rather mundane reports into romantic, exciting and extremely interesting events. I realised that if I wished to enjoy and appreciate Sorenson's work to the full, I would have to read the book in easy stages. This was something to look forward to. It would indeed be enjoyable to sit back and read a good book as the plane flew to South America. Although I had only two days to go before my flight, I succumbed to curiosity and dipped into the book from time to time as I finalised my programme prior to 'lift off'.

I must admit to being uncharitable towards my friends during this short period. Anything or anybody that prevented me having a sly look became irksome and seemed to put an intolerable strain on my social etiquette. It had reached the stage when Big Mac from the CID had visited me with a present and finding me unresponsive, had ironically asked: 'Oh what's wrang, what can a dae for yi, ma wee man?' My immediate reaction to his sarcasm was to tell him to depart to the nether regions, but knowing I was in the wrong, I apologised for my bad behaviour, informing him that as I was leaving shortly for the Americas, I had a lot on my mind. Accepting my apology with a grin, he asked me if I would be kind enough to open the parcel in his presence. When I opened the box, I recognised his present as a modern type of body warmer with metallic looking strips criss-crossing the fabric. My puzzled look spurred Big Mac to explain that I was looking at the latest and most effective bullet proof vest in existence. Tapping his nose, he assured me that it was my size and added that he wanted me to wear it during my sojourn in South America. Mimicking his Scot's tongue, I responded: 'Dinna be daft Mac, a'm no sodger, a'm only a foreign correspondent for a newspaper.'

The big man was not amused and proceeded to enlighten me regarding the facts of life, or death, in the bandit-infested territories of that rather beautiful but explosive continent. 'Chust you watch your step, Wil. The trouble in South America is being fired by the cartel that was headed by Jehu Cristo while in London.' His hesitation was dramatic before he unloaded his final warning. 'I haff chust found out that Jehu Cristo was assassinated for his failure while in Britain.' He was sure that the cartel would know by now that I had played a prominent part in exposing, and thereby causing, the failure of their plans. I balked at the suggestion of wearing the garment, but promised that if things got out of hand, I would use the vest. Big Mac shook his head, riposting: 'Put the vest on each day and keep death at bay.'

Despite all interruptions, I was almost halfway through the book as I boarded the plane and felt that Will Light was a far better man than I could ever expect to be. I marvelled at Sorenson's compassion and acute understanding of the human mind. Even his original villain, Lucius Chancitt, was not beyond redemption, if one conceded that at the height of his wrongdoing he had already become addicted to the poison he peddled and would suffer the same lingering and painful death as his victims. His message was clear to all who read his book: that drug addiction not only warped the mind, it also destroyed the human frame. As an afterthought, he added that although such addiction was small in percentage terms in relation to the total human race, three out of four drug peddlers could expect to die from drug addiction themselves. Where he obtained his statistics from I will never know, but his language was so rivetting, I felt it might curb the tendency of greedy social misfits risking their lives on what is known in the filthy trade as the 'quick fix'.

Some sensitive creatures might deplore what they considered as doom and gloom, but in the main his story was full of life and reflected the mind of a man who not only loved his fellows but also felt the need to entertain. He was determined as a 'wordsmith' to advance the cause of human need and happiness as opposed to greed and premature death. What intrigued me was Sorenson's artistry in balancing the teaching and at the same time thrilling his audience without sermonising in any way. What did disturb me somewhat was a reference to Will Light and Chanceet as they rallied the villagers and successfully fought off the bandit hirelings of the drug cartel. In the story Will, foreign correspondent of an influential London newspaper, had appealed for support in the fight against the drug barons. They had afterwards made representations to both governments. The Colombian Government had sent a token force of soldiers to the area and the British government, accepting warily that one of their nationals was involved, had indicated that they would be making enquiries in due course.

To me the situation was uncanny. After all, my brief was to discover what was really happening in Colombia and here in

Sorenson's book he had pre-empted the newspapers by almost a month. Turning the page, I discovered that a fortnight after the villagers had dispersed the bandits, Will had been taken prisoner under cover of darkness. It was a strange feeling, comparing myself with a fictional character, but under the circumstances I felt he should at least have been switched on. The bandits had roughed him up, then after chaining him, warned him that unless he answered certain questions he would be tortured in the morning. I was not too perturbed as I read on, but was relieved to find that Chanceet and his men had burst in on the bandit's camp and rescued Will. The author had seen fit to make Chanceet a real folk hero and in my estimation I felt sure he would succeed. There was little doubt in my mind that this book would become a classic in the not too distant future.

As for Will Light, this mercurial character who was prone to take unnecessary risks had been classified as a newspaper man. During the cocaine wars his life had been saved by Chanceet and he had declared he was prepared if necessary to die in Chanceet's struggle against the cocaine bandits. It was almost as if Sorenson was encouraging me, through his novel, to join with Chanceet and his people in their fight for freedom. This was, and had been, in my mind for a long time, but I knew it would not happen in the romantic fashion of a Sorenson novel. I needed no encouragement. After all, Chanceet had saved my life and that is a debt one carries through to the end of time. My editor had asked that I should investigate and report back on the unrest and revolts taking place in South America. Although my remit was far-reaching, it was my intention to join up with Chanceet as soon as possible. His village was approximately forty kilometres away from a port that had established itself as a smugglers' paradise. It was natural, therefore, that when the plane landed I should make tracks for that port of destiny.

This was the time for serious thought. If I really wanted to help my friend, I had to be a realist. I had no urge to become a dead hero. Thinking again about Will Light reminded me that in real life, these days, foreign correspondents were being captured and held hostage by the so-called freedom fighters and bandits. Ransom was then demanded from the governments of the nationals they held prisoner. Knowing what the present Government thought of me, I was sure they would be only too pleased to pay a handsome ransom, provided I was accidentally killed. It was therefore imperative to ensure I did not don the mantle of Will Light, but be myself and remain alive by using the wile and guile that had so often saved me in the past. I was at ease now. I knew what I had to do and even had time to reflect on Sorenson's work.

Having now read both novels, I felt inclined to favour *Chanceet* as opposed to *Sorenson*. They were both excellent in their own fashion, but whereas Sorenson was involved in many thrilling but questionable adventures, Chanceet was in effect a living legend who had saved his villagers from the clutches of the cocaine millionaires and shown by example that drug addiction could be conquered and that drug smugglers could be eliminated. My reflections, I have to admit, are a little naive, but I did feel that Sorenson's literary composition was such that it would be read worldwide and understood by many.

By the time I reached Bogota in Colombia, I was becoming restive and anxious concerning Chanceet's welfare. It would take another two days to reach the coast. It was my intention to make for the bay of Buenaventura and seek out the small fishing village I was particularly interested in. I wished to learn as much as I could regarding the habits and methods of the smugglers in that bay of 'good and profitable' adventure and then travel to Chanceet's village in the hinterland. I could only trust he was still alive and his enemies had been summarily dealt with.

I knew our meeting would be a joyous occasion and even if

the hirelings of the cocaine cartel had still to be dealt with, I would do my bit. I think I am like the average person concerning death and feel that a premature exit is a wasted resource. I am not a philosopher and find it difficult to understand the premise that it is only the good that die young. On this assumption, I feel somewhat confused but comforted, knowing that my 'sell by' date has been extended many times and yet I still consider that I'm not all that bad. I entered the small fishing village, having in mind the various ploys I would adopt in acquiring information that could be of value to Chanceet in his drive against drug smuggling. I was agreeably surprised to find that the fisher folk regarded him as a local hero, despite the distance of the hinterland from the sea. But I did make the mistake of casually asking a couple of sailors for their opinion regarding drug smuggling. In a flash the sailor nearest me had pinned my wrist to the table and his knife was too close to my throat for comfort. Giving him a sickly smile, I asked him what was wrong, while in my free hand I held my drink, hoping and praying I would not have to dampen his spirit before he attempted to kill me. My guardian angel, in the guise of a hefty man of the soil, stepped in just in time. Gripping my potential assailant's wrist, he delicately removed the offending instrument and chastised his countryman for his ungentlemanly conduct. Taking the sailors aside, he appeared to lecture them on proper social behaviour and then, returning to my table, assured me I would be quite safe, indicating that changes had taken place over the past two years. As I attempted to explain, he smiled and admitted he knew I was a friend of Chanceet but warned me against talking loosely about drugs.

As he left me I felt nervous, but had no need to do so, for he had left instructions that they were to look after me. What he had said to them I will never know, but within minutes I had become a legendary figure who had in the past played an important part in the life of their champion, Chanceet. The fisher folk were so friendly I felt almost a hostage to their hospitality. It took me two days to convince them that they were too kind, but having travelled a great distance, I was sure that Chanceet would be expecting me. They reluctantly accepted my plea but insisted I should travel to the hinterland in Emilio's taxi. I had done the journey before but in the opposite direction on the back of a Bolivian burro. Then it had been a dangerous undertaking, travelling through mountain passes, always keyed up and wondering if and when we might have to fight for survival against bloodthirsty bandits or other ill-mannered misfits. It was different this time as I sat in front with Emilio and enjoyed a not too bumpy passage. Instead of a donkey track, a narrow road with passing places had been hewn out of the mountain rock, reminding me of some of the old roads in the Western Highlands of Scotland. Two hours later Emilio stopped the car at a rather unpretentious villa and unloaded my belongings. As I turned to pay him, he smiled, shook his head, and before I could stop him, he was off. I had barely time to turn before Chanceet had lifted me and was hugging away in a bear-like fashion, leaving me little option but to reciprocate for my own safety. As he relaxed and allowed my feet to return to earth, he clapped me on the back and asked what had delayed me. I was too breathless to answer immediately and he was too excited to wait for a reply. 'You were in the fishing village two days ago.' Caught unawares, I asked how he knew. 'Pepe told me,' was his reply.

I was about to ask who Pepe was when I realised there was a big man standing beside him, the man who had intervened in the taverna in what might have been a rather messy affair. He smiled to me and addressed Chanceet. 'I saw Senor Ling in the Taverna and told him he would be safe in the fishing village. The villagers have obviously persuaded him to stay awhile.' Chanceet looked admiringly at his second in command and replied, 'Good for you, Pepe. I appreciate your effort in conveying to visitors that this part of Colombia is safe for honest people.' That evening was one of happy reunion with both of us recounting events that had taken place since we were last together. I enquired tentatively regarding any trouble they might have had recently from marauding gangsters or bandits. Chanceet pointed to Pepe, who was only too pleased to tell me that there had been no trouble for the past two years. Chanceet was proud of his young companion and was eager to recall his exceptional prowess in protecting the community from the attention of armed marauders and any criminal elements in the area between the fishing village and the hinterland. It was significant that the last raid had been a disaster for the marauders.

Pepe, a young Colombian, had, along with his parents, emigrated to America. As a young man he had passed through military school with flying colours and had seen service in action against guerillas and bandits, thus learning to cope with unorthodox warfare in the country and suburbia. Some two hundred and fifty heavily armed horsemen had swept through the village firing indiscriminately into the homes of the inhabitants. Then reversing, they had swept back down again hoping to finish their deathly task. The marauders had, however, been unaware of Pepe's skill as a strategist and tactician. He had ensured that scouts were positioned at strategic points equipped to signal swiftly the approach of potential enemies. The villagers, having been drilled, had taken effective cover in their houses as soon as the alarm sounded and a dozen trained men, from the cover of their bolt holes, had fired their machine guns into the galloping mass. Within five minutes more than a hundred horsemen were dead and the remainder were pleading for mercy as they lay entangled with their dead companions and writhing horse flesh. Pepe, a virile young man of strong character, had been deeply affected by the raid and displayed his compassion.

'It was terrible, Senor,' he said, 'to think that horses had to die or be maimed to satisfy the greed and cruelty of wicked and thoughtless men.' To me all the signs indicated there would be peace for a long time to come. I could be called selfish, but I did feel comforted and relaxed, knowing I might not have to try on Big Mac's present for size.

During the day I accompanied Chanceet as he made his rounds of the village and nearby environs, helping and encouraging his people in their communal tasks and advising those aspiring to higher educational levels. In the evening after dinner we reminisced, recalling both the hazardous and happy periods of our lives. Chanceet was particularly interested in learning as much as he could about Lucius Chancitt, the father he had never seen. He thanked me for being so candid, admitting his mother had been right in branding him as a scoundrel who had deserted her in her hour of need. Although reasonably proficient in Spanish and Portuguese, I had in the past had difficulty in understanding the Colombian idiom of Chanceet's hinterland, just as he had experienced a similar situation when I tried to converse with him in English. This time we were on even terms, due to both of us having in the past learned that the desire to understand overcomes all barriers. Having taught each other and found that we had a common aim in life, it was only natural to speculate on the future. As we talked, I had a strange but pleasant feeling that I was nearing a point in life when a major decision might have to be taken.

I am not a professional psychologist, but as an investigative journalist, I have over the years found it necessary to try and read the minds of men, and can only attribute my survival to the fact that I developed this sense fairly early on in my rather hazardous career. But what I now read was the desire for companionship between us. Chanceet was in his mid-eighties now but his strong frame and lively mind gave indications that he might not wish to retire before he had reached his century. He looked at me appealingly as he spoke. 'We have learned a lot from each other, Wil, and together we have in our own way fought with a measure of success against the intolerance, greed and cruelty of men.' As I nodded, he put his hand on my arm and, looking me straight in the eye, spoke huskily: 'I cherish your companionship, Wil, and ask that you seriously consider making our valley your home.' The atmosphere of warmth and friendship was such that I knew it was a message from the heart. Although I felt like accepting on the spot, my reply must have sounded somewhat prosaic to his ears. 'Your offer is indeed an honour, but it is one I would, in all fairness, wish to consider in some depth.' Chanceet seemed pleased and asked that we should discuss his suggestion from time to time. I was happy in his company and valued his companionship, but felt I was not quite ready for retirement. Later he countered that I, as a journalist, was performing an invaluable task in exposing corruption and in helping the authorities in the fight against drug smuggling and other evils. 'But,' he said, 'your contribution, although important, is small when considered on a worldwide scale, whereas here, your talents would be recognised in a more intimate and friendly society.'

On the fourth day he demonstrated some of the qualities that had made him the leader of his people. I had given him Sorenson's book to read and it was now obvious he had read the book from cover to cover. In his estimation Sorenson was not only an exceptional story teller, but was also extremely clever, appearing to have the power to forecast the future. When he referred to Will Light, I felt constrained and pointed out that I would have been more alert and not put my friends at hazard in effecting my escape. He smiled broadly and agreed. 'Probably, Wil, but remember there was a time when you were a prisoner and I your guard. Fortunately for both of us, we had a common interest in

137

humanity. We both learned a lot while we were together and I'm sure we have both done our share towards making the world a more tolerable place in which to live.'

There was more to come and as it developed I felt increasingly that Sorenson had indeed put me on the spot. He referred to the achievements of Will Light and particularly to the significant part he had played in the economy of the valley. 'Sorenson was not only a good author, Wil, but knowing that vital stages of your life have been enacted in Colombia, especially in this beautiful valley of ours, he has seen fit to clothe Will Light in all the attributes you possess.' Chanceet then reeled off parts of my life, such as my adventures as a foreign correspondent and investigative journalist, even my experience as an engineer and trade union official. As I pondered his view of things, he advanced his theory a little further: 'I'm not saying Sorenson is clever just because he cast me as an extraordinary folk hero, but I do know that he really believes your love of this valley is such that you have given thought to settling here, hopefully enjoying my companionship and, if so inclined, using your talents in advancing the social and economic wellbeing of our people.' I nodded agreement and asked him to relax; there was no need for him to encourage me to live in the valley. Although I did not envisage retirement, I did feel a desire to join him in his noble venture. However, I had been given an assignment which I had to honour and it was my intention to leave for Bogota the following day.

He smiled but looked perplexed when I told him I had been sent to cover the sporadic revolutions in South America and their probable connections with the drug trade. For a moment he was silent, then laughed and offered his opinion. 'Of course you must do your job, Wil, but I would ask you to relax now. It is true that some months ago some small rebellions did take place, but since then only minute spasms have disturbed the peace.' Realising I was serious, he asked me to accompany him to his command centre. From his villa he took me to a solid concrete structure in which were stored automatic weapons and other rather nasty pieces of military equipment. He felt an explanation was in order. 'It is just too bad, Wil. Let's hope it will not be too long before these death machines can be turned into ploughshares.' We passed through a door into a small office containing all the equipment necessary for it to function as a communications centre.

Seated in the centre was Pepe and he was busy on the telephone, an instrument I knew to have been foreign to the valley the last time I had visited Chanceet. Seeing my bewilderment, he took full advantage. 'So you see, Wil, you could phone your boss from here.' I thanked him but declined his offer, knowing that I had to be firm. Thinking I was being clever, I suggested there was a difference between 'modus operandi' and 'modus vivendi'. Chanceet smiled and pointed to his collection of books. I could see he had built up a considerable library and the English section occupied more space than I would have expected. 'A long time ago, Wil, when you were teaching me the English language, I vowed I would learn not only the language but also the customs of your country. I do know that 'modus operandi' is the method of working while 'modus vivendi' is a mode or way of living, but I also remember you saying that it is more important to learn how to live in harmony with your fellow men than it is to seek an advantage in the world of business.' Admitting intellectual defeat, I had little option but to resort to the mundane and explain that as my assignment had been planned to start from Bogota, it was essential I should at least be there to receive instructions and report back to base. He was magnanimous and let me off the hook. 'I know how you feel, Wil. You have already made an appointment and must keep it, but remember, now that you know I have a telephone, I expect you to ring me in the not too distant future.' As I nodded and promised, he added, 'Make this your home, Wil, this is where you belong.'

In the morning Emilio took me to the harbour and an hour later I was on my way to Bogota. As I checked in at the hotel, the receptionist seemed unduly relieved. 'The hotel is happy to see you, sir. For two days we have had messages by telephone from a man called editor. He lives in London, England, and he is telling me about the morning sun and we know there is much fog and snow there now.' As I thanked him, he put his finger to his forehead and asked, 'Is he loco, sir?' I shrugged my shoulders and, thanking him for his patience, took my key and made for the lift. Halfway across the hall I heard a call: 'Senor Ling.' As I turned, I saw the receptionist holding the telephone and covering the mouthpiece. 'Senor Ling, important call from London. As I advanced towards him, he took his hand off the mouthpiece and putting his finger to the side of his head made what he considered to be the appropriate sign. It was, of course, my dear old editor and, hoping to stymie him, I commiserated, 'Terrible weather you are having over there.' His riposte almost seared my delicate ears: 'Never mind the bloody weather, where the hell have you been for the last three days?' I did not attempt to explain or make excuses, I did as I have always done, I waited patiently, allowing his safety valve to operate until the steam dried up. Having reached that stage, I was still forbearing, again attempting to answer his original question. A sudden gasp or spasm at the other end indicated I would have to be firm. My reply was straight to the point 'If you don't allow me to speak, I will just hang up.' When I had told him that I had discovered that the revolution had fizzled out, he blurted back: 'Well, what the hell is the idea of wasting time in Colombia when there is a real threat of revolution over here in London?'

As I pleaded ignorance of the present state of affairs in the British Isles, the editor almost hysterically outlined what was happening. After years of blundering along, the Government had at last lost all credibility. The 'sleaze factor' or 'chairman's disease' had increased dramatically and the workers were preparing for a national strike. No longer prepared to accept the diktat of London, the Scots had elected their own government and had already applied for membership of the European Common Market. Feeling he had ultimately reached a stage where I could intervene, I asked if I could say something. Reluctantly he agreed and I asked, 'So what?' 'So what?' he bellowed. 'It means your services are required in London. We need someone like you to nose out some of the bigger bastards among the "sleazers".' In the end I said I would give the matter serious consideration. The editor, my boss, always a fair man, gave me a deadline. 'If you are not back here in three days time, you can consider that you will no longer enjoy your position on the *Morning Sun*.'

That evening I took things easy in the lounge and read all the newspapers I could lay my hands on. I found the editor had indeed been correct in his assumption, it certainly did appear that this decadent, dissolute and destructive government was at last on its way out. It in no way comforted me that this so-called government. would go down in history as the most inefficient administration of the twentieth century. I could only feel sorry for those who were expected to pick up the pieces. One thing was certain: I would not be one of them. I felt I had done my bit in exposing their sleazy ploys and greedy masters. I felt I was now free to enjoy making a contribution to the advancement of the people of the hero who had saved my life.

In the morning I thought it only fair that the editor should know how I felt and I telephoned him accordingly. I told him, 'Having given serious thought and consideration to all the information imparted yesterday, I cannot accept that anything has really changed. From 1979 onwards we have had government by decree; the idea that we had any semblance of democracy is indeed laughable. The propaganda and policy of the ruling class has been one of greed and the 'devil take the hindmost'. Having

141

done my little bit in exposing these merchants of sleaze, I can well understand that the Scots no longer wish to be chained to the London business machine. I have therefore decided that there is no point in trying to comfort myself in the rays of the *Morning Sun*.' My boss, a Scottish schemer and a very efficient one at that, had another go and after playing around with words like loyalty and wisdom, he dealt his last card. 'Guid luck to you, laddie,' he said. 'I understand how you feel but I forgot to tell you there is a snap election tomorrow and although the press is sure the Conservatives will be booted out, the country is in such a mess that the incoming government could be faced with an almost impossible task in restoring the economy and credibility of the country.' There was a crackling sound as communication was cut for several minutes, then he came back loud and clear. 'And you know how fickle the public can be. Even this lot of Tory idiots could be returned before the year is out.'

But he had been too crafty this time. Hoping to entice me back quickly, he was banking on my aptitude for exposing sleaze and corruption in our rotten system and of course the headlines it provided. Unfortunately for him he was really looking backwards, while I was planning forwards, looking towards my future. His voice was a little strained as he asked, 'Well, what do you think, Wil?' I thought it only courteous to reply, 'I thank you for your observations and having clarified how you feel concerning the possibility of another objectionable Tory administration being elected in the near future, I can only offer my condolences. However, it has certainly been instrumental in determining my future plans.'

Before he could ask me about my plans for the future, I rang off and immediately rang Chanceet's number, wondering as I dialled if he would be in his study or walking around the farms in that beautiful hinterland valley. It was wonderful to hear the voice of my old friend and after the usual pleasantries, I committed myself. 'I'm coming home, Chanceet, I have missed you.' For a minute there was silence then his voice came over loud and clear: 'Welcome home, Wil, I will go and prepare a place for you.'